"Run, Blythe, now!"

Blythe wanted to stay near Simms, but he shoved her. "Go to the vehicle and get in." She heard the beep from his key fob. "It's unlocked."

He shoved the fob in her hand. "If anything happens, you drive yourself out of here."

"I can't drive."

"You'll learn."

Blythe took off, the rain pouring over her like sheets of ice. She slipped as gunshots pinged all around her. She didn't dare glance back. Simms had told her to keep running.

Out of breath, she reached the SUV and jumped into the driver's seat.

How did she crank the thing?

When she heard more gunshots, she searched the steering wheel and saw a wide slit. Testing the fob, she cried out when it went right into the base of the steering wheel.

So now all she had to do was crank the SUV and drive out of the parking spot. But what happened after that?

The passenger door swung open, causing her to let out a scream.

"Drive," Simms said, his gun aimed behind him. "They're coming for us."

With over seventy books published and millions in print, **Lenora Worth** writes award-winning romance and romantic suspense. Three of her books finaled in the ACFW Carol Awards, and her Love Inspired Suspense novel *Body of Evidence* became a *New York Times* bestseller. Her novella in *Mistletoe Kisses* made her a *USA TODAY* bestselling author. Lenora goes on adventures with her retired husband, Don, and enjoys reading, baking and shopping...especially shoe shopping.

Visit the Author Profile page at LoveInspired.com for more titles.

UNDERCOVER IN AMISH COUNTRY

LENORA WORTH

LOVE INSPIRED SUSPENSE
INSPIRATIONAL ROMANCE

LOVE INSPIRED® SUSPENSE
INSPIRATIONAL ROMANCE

ISBN-13: 978-1-335-63871-7

Recycling programs for this product may not exist in your area.

Undercover in Amish Country

Copyright © 2025 by Lenora H. Nazworth

Love Inspired
22 Adelaide St. West, 41st Floor
Toronto, Ontario M5H 4E3, Canada
www.LoveInspired.com

Printed in U.S.A.

Thou art my hiding place; thou shalt preserve me
from trouble; thou shalt compass me about
with songs of deliverance.
—*Psalm* 32:7

To all the people who helped me get this book
finished. It went through several changes
and I went through all the emotions, but here it is.
Thank you to my editors and my longtime
writer friends for helping me tell Simms's story.
I hope it was worth the wait.

ONE

The cold air slapped at her with an icicle sharpness. Blythe Meissner ignored the icy sting. Her numb fingers gripped her backpack straps, and her wool cape lifted as she ran into the frigid woods near her home in Campton Creek, Pennsylvania. Her heart burned a heated pulse with each step she took, the frigid snow so deep it hit the top of her winter boots. But she kept going.

She'd been right all along. Someone was after her again. She had not imagined all the strange happenings around here—the missing items from her chifforobe, the kitchen being rearranged and footsteps kicking around outside her window. Her *Aenti* Rita seemed to think she was having flashbacks of the horror she'd endured over a year ago when her husband, Hayden Meissner, had held her hostage in a shack in a Florida swamp.

Thinking of her husband made Blythe's panic return full force. Was he tormenting her from prison? She'd married Hayden four years ago thinking she'd have a good life and be able to get away from her resentful *aenti*'s constant wrath. But she'd gone from bad to worse when Hayden had moved her to Pinecraft, Florida, and she'd become a prisoner in her own home after finding out he wasn't just the owner of a successful propane company. Her older husband had been involved in price-gouging and smuggling, along with other crimes, including murdering those who crossed him. And she'd been the one to bring him down with evidence she'd found on a flash drive.

After it was all over, drained and defeated, she'd decided to leave Pinecraft and come home, hoping to find forgiveness with the community she loved. But now, she wasn't so sure about staying in Campton Creek.

I won't think about that. I won't. He's in prison and he'll be there for a long time.

Hayden was imprisoned in a New York facility not far from where she lived. Too close for comfort or coincidence. Now she imagined a hundred different ways he could have bribed a judge or the prison warden. Hayden had ways of getting what he wanted with either money or threats. Or worse.

She'd testified against him.

Shivering, Blythe remembered the last time

she'd looked into his evil black eyes. He wouldn't forget what she'd done.

Tonight, she'd realized her worst nightmare had returned.

Hayden Meissner wanted her dead. He'd made that clear the day the jury had convicted him.

"You'll regret this, Blythe. I gave you the world, you ungrateful, confused girl. You will wish you hadn't turned on me."

Blythe pushed the image of him turning in handcuffs to scream at her out of her mind. She stopped by a towering oak tree to catch her breath, the last rays of the feeble sun moving through the trees while darkness stalked her with shadows. She couldn't have a panic attack now, not out here all alone and when someone followed her every step. She'd come home from working at the general store only to hear someone rumbling around in the home she shared with *Aenti* Rita and *Aenti*'s new husband, Arthur.

They were away visiting his family.

So who had been in her house earlier?

She'd run away when she heard two men whispering. They'd likely seen her out the window but she'd kept running toward the shortcut to the township proper. She'd go to the police station.

Could she make it before they found her?

Taking a deep breath, she tried to calm herself. She'd get help. She'd get away. She would not go through what she'd endured with Hayden. He'd tried to kill her and he'd tormented her sister Adina when Adina had come to Pinecraft to search for Blythe. Now Adina was safe and living in Pinecraft, happily married to Nathan Kohr.

Blythe wanted nothing of marriage.

I can't marry anyone because I can't trust any man. And because she was still married to Hayden. Forever. The laws of her faith maintained she couldn't remarry unless he died. But there were no laws regarding how he'd kill her first just to get even. Nothing would stop him. But why now? Had he been biding his time? Making big plans. Did he have another woman waiting in the wings?

I won't let it happen. He can't torment me anymore.

She repeated a silent prayer over and over as she listened to the sound of birds rustling in the trees, the push of the chilling wind hitting her cheeks and the roar of vehicle engines up on the main highway. Nothing else. No footsteps, no voices. Maybe she'd overreacted. Gripping her backpack, she thought some habits never died. She'd always carried a backpack, and the one she'd sent to Adina had held information that saved their lives and put her husband away. Glad she had a new one with her now, containing money and a burner phone. Two things she was never without these days, because she was so terrified of what might happen. Of what was possibly happening right now.

Blythe walked in a hurry, her sturdy brown winter boots hitting against bramble and stones of the thicket path, headed toward the township proper. She hoped the authorities would believe her and help her.

Then she heard a pounding sound. Footsteps crashing through the shrubs, voices echoing out over the forest. They were coming after her. She ran into the woods and held herself against a massive tree, trying not to breathe, her pulse so swift and jittery she was sure they could hear it rushing through her body.

Slowly, she pivoted behind the huge tree trunk and looked west toward town, but as she turned to run in that direction, she came face-to-face with a big hulking man wearing a dark cap.

He grinned. "There you are. You think you're smart, but we gotcha now."

Blythe darted left and tried to run but the man came after her, calling out, "We'll take care of you and it'll be over. Your husband is dead. Died in prison two days ago. We just need to talk to you about a few loose ends he didn't get to tie up."

She stopped, gasping. "Hayden is dead?" Why hadn't someone alerted her? Had she missed a message in the phone booth out on the road? Could it be true?

One of the men sneered at her question. "Yes. You have nothing to fear from him."

Blythe didn't believe the giant trying to corner her. "But I do need to fear you two."

She turned to get away but saw the other man heading toward her like a bull about to attack. He tripped over a knotted limb covered with snow, giving her time to escape.

But the big man behind her rushed up and stood in her path.

Blythe screamed as he pushed toward her and knocked her over. Her backpack went skidding out of sight while she tried to scoot away.

He grabbed her booted foot. "We mean you no harm. We need to take you to someone who wants to talk to you."

"Neh!" she shouted into the growing darkness, pushing and kicking, her hands burning from hitting against cold, jagged stones buried under the snow. She felt a wet stone beneath her hand and managed to dig it out of the damp earth and snow. It fit her hand like a baseball. With a grunt and a prayer, she aimed it toward the man's forehead with a swift whack. He went down, moaning as he let go of her boot, profanity spewing from his mouth.

That gave her enough time to push up on her

elbows, roll away from him, grab her backpack and run into the trees. She knew the path, but they didn't. Distracted, the two men argued and mumbled while she hurried with all her might to the road up ahead, her lungs burning with fear and panic, her eyes misting as the cold hit her face with a relentless moisture.

She couldn't stay here. She'd go back to Florida and hide at her sister's place for a few days. No one would even know she was there.

And she'd find the one man who could protect her.

Detective Simon Bueller, or Simms as he was called, the man who'd stayed with her at the hospital, who'd talked to her when she'd woken up screaming, the man who'd guarded her and reluctantly held her hand when she had nightmares—he would protect her. Over the weeks after they'd found her, she'd relived each moment of being kidnapped by her husband and kept in a shack in the swamp, but Simms had tolerated her fears and anxieties with a quiet strength. At the age of thirty, he was five years older than Blythe, but they had become close, almost friends, and yet she hadn't even told him goodbye when she'd left. Simms had done his job. And she had come home to find forgiveness and peace.

Too much trauma, too much between them, even if the attraction had been immediate.

They were both broken and shattered, so things couldn't go beyond a tentative friendship.

Besides, she had still been married when she'd come home to Campton Creek. Blythe stumbled and stopped. One of those men had told her Hayden was dead. If that were true, she was a widow now. Everything had changed.

But Simms had left the Amish long ago, and that would never change. Besides, she didn't need him for anything other than helping her stop these threats. He was *gut* at his job—that she knew, but she also knew how she'd felt when he'd held her hand in the hospital.

Instead of going to the local police, she ran toward the bus station to buy a ticket south, and prayed she'd make it to him before someone tried to take her again.

Sarasota Detective Simon Bueller didn't like being woken up in the middle of the day, mainly because he never slept well and he did a lot of surveillance—all night long. When he had an opportunity to sleep, he wanted to sleep. He did not want to be disturbed. Last night had been a tough one, with a drug bust and a teenager who'd overdosed on some sort of magic cocktail. He wasn't ready to wake up to the troubles of the world.

So he ignored the buzz of his cell phone.

When it rang for the fourth time, he groaned

as he rolled over, mumbled underneath his breath and answered it with a snarl. He'd been asleep almost all day. Now the sun was hovering over the Gulf of Mexico right outside the open sliding door of his cottage.

"Simms. And this had better be really important."

"I'm in trouble."

He knew that voice. Had heard the alluring huskiness of it in his dreams. Wide awake now, he heaved a huff of breath. "Blythe?"

"Someone is after me, Simms. They told me Hayden is dead. They chased me into the woods."

He stood, looking for clothes and grabbing his gun off the nightstand. "Where are you now?"

"At the bus station in Pinecraft. When I got home from work a couple nights ago, two men tried to attack me. I ran to the woods and got away. I got on a bus and left Campton Creek in the middle of the night and transferred to another bus in Atlanta. It's happening again, Simms."

Simms hissed a breath. What was going on with this woman? Would she ever find peace? She'd been terrified, but she'd testified against her husband only to hear him shouting threats at her as they carted him away. Had he carried through on those threats?

"Go inside the church," he told her. "I'm on my way."

She didn't say anything, but the fear in her voice curled around him like a tightening chain. He'd known *of* Blythe Meissner before ever getting involved in bringing her husband to justice.

But once he heard her story from her own lips and in her own words, he began to see he'd misjudged the young woman. The older man she'd married was evil all wrapped up in the guise of being a staunch Amish businessman with a propane empire. He didn't know the meaning of faith, and he sure hadn't respected his marriage vows or his wife.

But dead? That was interesting. Of course, Meissner had many enemies. If he'd sent someone after Blythe as he'd promised in the courtroom, how had he wound up dead?

"Blythe, don't go anywhere, you hear me? I'll call a patrol car to come and stay with you until I can get into town."

"I'm sorry, Simms. I'm sure you thought you were through with me."

"Not by a long shot," he said, meaning it. "I'm on my way."

He'd had mixed feelings about Blythe Maas Meissner. She was a dark-haired beauty and she was also trouble. Or she had been when she was the high-and-mighty wife of a wealthy Amish man.

When he'd last seen her, she'd been a shell

of that woman, more subdued, meek and mild, timid almost. He'd kind of missed the old Blythe. He could now admit to himself that he was attracted to her, but he didn't need that kind of distraction. And besides, he was not Amish anymore.

She let out a sob, bringing him back to reality, then she whispered, "I'm scared."

"I know you are, but I'll be there soon."

He hung up, got into the vintage muscle car he'd been working on for years, and shifted the gears to full throttle. Being a detective in Sarasota, Florida, kept him busy enough, but he watched over the Amish community of Pinecraft because even though he'd left the Amish years ago, he could still keep the small community safe. Especially when it got crowded during the winter months. Could he keep Blythe safe?

Blythe back in Pinecraft.

And Hayden Meissner dead?

Hope warred with frustration as Simms zoomed through the quiet streets and called for backup as he went. If Hayden had died—or been murdered—in prison, then who was after Blythe?

It would be his job to find that out.

Blythe had caved and called Simms first. Before she'd gone to her sister's house. Only because on the long bus ride here, she'd decided she wouldn't put Adina and her new family in danger. If she showed up there, and these people saw her, they'd harass the Kohr family. She couldn't put them through fearing for their lives again.

So that left Simms. If they were careful, her sister wouldn't know about any of this until they'd stopped it cold.

Simms could do that. He was a *gut* lawman. Before she'd married Hayden, Blythe knew little about criminals and the law, only what she'd read in books or heard in passing while watching the television at the general store. Now she knew more about those subjects than she'd ever wanted to know.

And she also knew Simms better than she'd ever expected. Even if she'd done all the talking, the man's eyes and body language had told her a lot. He was tormented, he was reckless and he wanted no part of the Amish community anymore.

And yet, he made it his business to protect the Amish in Pinecraft.

Standing here now in the gloaming as the sun went away, covered in a dark bonnet and heavy black cape, she hoped she looked like any Amish woman waiting to be picked up at the bus station. A few people mingled around and waited for cabs, but soon everyone would be gone and she'd be alone. She remembered Adina waiting here for Blythe to come and pick her up, but Hayden's people had held Blythe and chased Adina. Which had led her sister right into Nathan's strong arms, thankfully. He and Adina made a *wunderbar* couple.

Blythe was happy for them. They now had one child and lived with Nathan's mother, Ruth, over her quilt shop, located on one of the busy streets around Pinecraft.

Blythe glanced at her surroundings. Adina's home wasn't far from here. Maybe she should just go there after all.

But no. Adina didn't need any of this in her life. And the less said now, the better. Especially since they'd all forgiven *Aenti* for siding with Hayden and telling him Adina had gone looking for Blythe. Blythe had to wonder though, if her *aenti* knew more about Hayden than she was saying. She seemed mighty keen on keeping up with him even when he was behind bars.

Aenti Rita had also asked for forgiveness for pushing Blythe off on a bad man, a powerful man who would give them all the life her *aenti* had dreamed of, the life Blythe had dreamed of, too. Now she only wanted a quiet life, and she'd worked hard to find her way back to her faith and her community.

Would all that end? Would she die even after trying to atone for her sins?

She glanced up and saw a shadow on the street. A lone man walking with purpose toward the bus station located in the parking lot of the Mennonite church used by the Amish who flocked to Pinecraft to get away from the cold up north.

The man was tall and he wore a denim jacket and dark pants, his black boots heavy and laced up to his calves. Scary and out of place here. Oh, no! She'd seen him get on the bus back in Atlanta. He'd sat up front and kept his head down, but she'd walked past him when they got off the bus.

Could he have followed *her* all this way?

Her first instinct was to run.

Simms had told her to stay so she stood and tried to melt into the building, her heart beating in fear, her prayers caught in her brain like twisted metal. She could be wrong. This man might be waiting for a ride. The man glanced up and scanned the area, his gaze finally landing on Blythe. She lowered her head and pretended to be reading a pamphlet she'd picked up earlier.

He started toward her, his eyes as dark as night, a smirk on his face, one hand reaching inside his jacket. She could see him coming underneath the shutters of her eyelashes.

Where was Simms? Where was the patrol car?

The man approached, determined, the heat of danger bouncing off him like a laser. Ten feet away, five feet away. No one around her.

He reached deep into his jacket and pulled out a gun with a slick long barrel. He aimed. Blythe froze, knowing she was about to die. Then she heard a car revving into the parking lot, tires screeching, a motor roaring like a lion. A man jumped out of the car and shouted, "Drop the gun. Now."

Simms!

The man who'd been about to shoot her turned and shot at Simms instead, but Simms shot back and the man went down like a black bird at her feet.

And he didn't move.

Blythe went blank, ignoring Simms's shouts for her to run. A siren shrilled through the night while people screamed and ran away. But she stood terrified, her mind trapped in the dark, damp space where her husband had held her. She couldn't move because she could remember the feel of the sticky grasping legs of spiders and bugs moving over her skin, could hear the rodents tapping away as they roamed around the dirt-covered, moldy floors and scooted over her dirty skirt.

Neh, You're not there in that shack. You're at the bus station and Simms is here.

The man lying two feet away from her grunted and flipped over, causing Blythe to let out a scream. Like a rocket being shot out of a cannon, he stood up and held onto his bleeding side as he ran off behind the church.

Still, Blythe couldn't say a word or move away. Her breath came in shallow waves, her damp cold hands shook, her heartbeat spiked and plunged, while the horrors of her past shadowed her like murky waters growing deeper and deeper.

A strong hand grabbed her arm. "Blythe?"

"*Neh*, let me go," she cried out, gasping. "*Neh*."

The man pivoted her around to face him and held her with both hands now. "Blythe, it's me. Simms. C'mon. We have to get you out of here."

She glanced up and into Simms's deep blue-black eyes that always reminded her of a raging sea. "You came."

"I said I would and here I am," he replied urging her toward his fancy car. "That one won't bother you again. He's shot and he won't make it far."

"Will he die?"

"No, but he'll be in such pain, he'll wish he could. I've got people out searching for him." He urged her across the parking lot while he kept her by his side. When they got to his car, he opened the car door and gently pushed her inside. After he had her safely in the car, he said, "You stay right here while I talk to the first responders." He pointed to the left. "I'll be a few feet away. Don't get out of the car."

Blythe nodded, too numb to move. Laying her head against the leather headrest, she inhaled the scents of leath-er polish and a spicy cologne, then closed her eyes and silently prayed, thanking the Lord for Simms arriving when he did.

A little while later, he came back and got into the car. "Hey, you okay?"

She gave him a long look, taking in his lush black shaggy hair and his sun-tanned face. She'd missed Simms and she'd missed this place. She could admit that now that she was back in Pinecraft. She'd gone home because she thought she belonged there. Self-punishment.

Now, she could almost breathe again.

"Hayden is dead," she said, the shock of that taking over her body and shattering her brief reprieve. "Dead, Simms."

Simms gave her a stoic stare. "I'll have to verify that, okay? I gave the other officers my statement and I'll take yours later. Let's get you out of here. Do you want to go to Adina's house?"

"*Neh*," she said, her throat muscles burning. "I don't want her involved. It's too dangerous.

She and Nathan have been through enough because of me. Take me to your house, Simms."

When he looked uncertain, she touched her hand to his. "Please."

Simms sat for a moment, his dark, brooding gaze telling her his thoughts were fighting a war—a war regarding what to do about her, the same war she'd fought with herself on so many sleepless nights. Then he gave her a look that held them both in suspension, as if they were dangling on a tight rope. She thought he'd say something but he nodded and cranked the purring car. They were off into the night, leaving behind the grisly scene at the bus station, leaving the lights of the city and the horror of this night, to be absorbed by the darkness of an old road that took them to a seaside cottage high up on pilings, where the waves from the Gulf of Mexico crashed angrily against the shore with a never-ending grace.

Despite her fears of what might come, she liked that Simms held her hand all the way there.

TWO

Simms had to wrap his brain around this situation. A beautiful woman with dark hair and deep brown eyes that flickered golden at times, a troubled, traumatized, terrified woman he'd tried to forget, was walking toward the balcony of his home on the water.

He watched as she opened the double glass doors and embraced the chilly air. Even though it was November, the weather on the peninsula of Florida rarely went beyond the freezing mark. Still, the wind could run a chill over even the toughest person.

He watched and wished and waited, his frigid heart melting with each sigh she took. He'd decided on a whim, when she was staying with her sister after Meissner's trial had ended, to go by and see how Blythe was doing. But he'd been too late. She'd already left and gone back to Campton Creek. He'd often wondered if they might have become friends. He was already a friend of Nathan's when he'd met Adina. That little woman had a lot of courage and might.

And so did her sister, who now stood taking in the night view. Blythe was back in his life and in a big way. Reminding himself that Blythe was frightened and still vulnerable, he pushed any attraction he might have far to the back side of his hard heart, and also reminded himself that she was forbidden.

Blythe was back because her life was in danger. He needed to remember his job. He needed to remember he didn't like to be distracted. He needed to remember so many things, but all he could think about right now was Blythe standing there looking so fragile and alone. He hoped she'd listen to his advice. His dad hadn't listened to him all those years ago and having someone from home here again only rattled his doubts and his grief.

"We do not fight," Daed kept repeating. "I did no wrong."

But the world hadn't believed his *daed*, who'd been accused of taking money from the Englisch farmer he worked for. By the time Simms had done some digging on his own and found out the man's son had stolen the money, it was too late. His father was never the same and neither was Simms. They argued and Simms left. To find justice. Always.

He'd do that again for Blythe.

But what was he to do with Blythe while they tried to figure this out. "It's still beautiful," she said when he moved toward the doors to pull her inside. "The way the moon glistens on the water and how the waves do that dance with the shore makes me feel so safe and cloistered." She glanced back at him. "Or it used to. Not so much after Hayden locked me up."

She'd told him about that. Being locked in her own beachside villa. She'd tried to escape only once, so to punish her, Meissner had moved her to an old shack in the swamps nearby.

The swamps—full of snakes, spiders, alligators and all kinds of predators. Human predators who'd guarded her and almost starved her to death.

"I want you to be safe here, Blythe," he said, letting his own dreams and nightmares wash away with the tug of water against the shore. "But we'll need to move you."

On the way here, he'd questioned her about what had happened in Campton Creek, and about the man tonight. She'd explained how one of the men told her about her husband's death and some loose ends that needed tying up.

She might be the only loose end they needed to get rid of.

"Move me?" She pivoted around and came inside, allowing him to close the doors and draw the heavy curtains across them. "Why?"

Simms ran a hand through his tousled hair. "Oh, several reasons. You're…a newly widowed woman, you're Amish, and it's not right our being together here alone."

"Aren't we past that, Simms?" She held up her hand when he tried to speak. "I don't mean anything inappropriate when I say that. You are the only person besides my sister and her husband that I feel I can trust. I don't care about being proper when someone is tormenting me and trying to kill me."

She had a valid point. He rolled it around in his tired brain. "I'll get a female officer to stay here with you at all times."

Blythe's dark eyebrows lifted up at that, her frown full of disappointment and despair. "Is it necessary?"

"Yes," he said, remembering how stubborn she could be. "I can't be here with you twenty-four seven. I need to report this to my captain and then I have to find out what's going on with your husband's death."

"I think he was murdered," she said, her voice a chilling calm. "I should be mourning him, but—"

"You can't, right?"

"I can't. He was pure evil. I won't shed a tear for him."

"Now someone is after you," he reminded her. "From what you've told me, Meissner could be behind this, or someone *did* murder him, and now they want you dead, too. They could want something from you, before they get rid of you. We just need to figure out the loose ends those guys mentioned to you."

"It could be someone carrying out his dying wish," she retorted. "He still torments me, dead or not dead."

Simms almost pulled her into his arms. Almost.

Instead he made her some tea he kept here for his sister, and had Blythe sit down on the couch, while he took an old, leather side chair.

"I'm sorry you're still dealing with this," he finally said. "I'll call headquarters and get someone out here to help."

Blythe nodded. "I suppose that is the best plan for now."

Then she glanced around. "I thought your house burned down after someone bombed the place."

"Things got messed up. The barn burned and the house got some damage," he replied. "I did a few renovations, upped security." He shrugged.

"I got shot a few weeks back, so I haven't finished the renovations on the barn."

"You get shot a lot, ain't so?"

Why she'd ask that now, when she was the one
in danger, he had no clue. Maybe she was afraid
he'd get killed and she'd have no one to protect
her. "Yeah. I've been on desk duty for a while,
recovering. But I'm better now."

Now he had a bone to chew, a case to solve.
The whole precinct would be glad to get him out
of their hair. Simms was not the desk-duty type.

Blythe fidgeted and picked up a huge conch
shell he'd left on a table. "Don't you get tired of
this, Simms? This living in the shadows, hiding
in plain sight, trying to stomp out all the evil in
the world."

"Every day," he admitted, his tone bordering
on exhaustion.

"Do you ever think of quitting?"

"Every day," he repeated. "But right now I
can't."

"Because of me." She stood and circled the
small, sparse den and then went to the kitchen
where she had another view of the water through
the massive window over the sink. "I've always
been trouble."

"I don't doubt it."

"You could have ignored my call."

"Nope, I'm afraid that would be impossible."

"Because you have a job to do."

He studied her for a moment, taking in the *kapp* covering all that silky hair, and the prim white apron over her dark wool winter dress. "Because you are impossible to ignore, Blythe."

Then he grabbed his phone. "I have to make some calls. You can take my sister's bedroom and bath." He pointed to the left. "The windows are bulletproof and the only way in is through me."

Blythe stood still, shock changing to acceptance while she gave him her Blythe-stare. A stare that could mess with a man's head. Then she nodded and picked up her floral backpack. The woman loved those things, and now her sister Adina carried one, too. But sending her sister a backpack with a flash drive hidden in its seam had saved the day with helping Simms and the department take down Hayden Meissner.

"Do you need clothes and supplies?" he asked, thinking she'd probably packed a lot of stuff.

"I might. I ran away with just this pack, but I keep money and a burner phone in it or I wouldn't have been able to get down here or call you."

"Smart," he said, admiring her tenacity. "I'm going to protect you, Blythe."

She turned, stared him down, then tilted her head to the side. "I won't go back into the swamps, Simms. I won't."

"Ain't gonna happen," he growled. "You're with me now."

Then he turned and headed to the small office in his bedroom.

Before he did something really stupid like hugging her. He couldn't do that because he was rusty in the giving comfort department. Blythe deserved more than he could ever offer, but the one thing he could offer her was protection.

For now.

Blythe couldn't sleep.

Why had she come here of all places? *Aenti* always said that her impulsiveness would get her into trouble.

Well, her *aenti* had been right. After Rita suggested to Blythe that she needed to get married and introduced her to Hayden, who needed a wife, she'd impulsively fallen for Hayden's charm and his wealth. He'd been powerful, which in Blythe's mind meant protection and security. Since she and Adina lost their parents at an early age, she'd never felt secure with family love and grace, or practical things such as money and food. And *Aenti* Rita had made it very clear that she didn't have much grace, but she did like money. She was mean, and even though she'd confessed to giving Hayden information about Adina and Blythe when Blythe had gone missing, she had tried to be a more docile, caring person. At least, she'd put up a good front.

Until she got married again. Her *aenti*, so bitter and spiteful, was now married to a man who, while not wealthy, seemed to have enough money to pacify Rita. Arthur Glick had shown up in Campton Creek last year. He worked for a big construction company and made a modest living. After a few weeks of making the rounds to get to know people, he'd taken to *Aenti* Rita's flirting and cooking—something she rarely enjoyed doing. Soon they were visiting after church and he began to go along with her to see other families—another thing she'd never enjoyed before. But she loved showing off her new beau.

They had married about four months ago, and they seemed happy. *Aenti* did not, however, like having Blythe in the house now that she had a husband. She'd gone back to her mean ways and the constant complaints of having to worry about her deceased sister's two girls. She'd told Arthur her version of "that horrible time." Meaning Hayden's evil ways and his jail sentence. It had almost ruined her life, Rita liked to say.

Blythe had been uncomfortable and in the way, so she kept to her room, reading books or the Bible and thinking about the world she'd left behind.

Now their *aenti* could live comfortably for

the rest of her life. But had Rita been just as impulsive as she accused Blythe of being? There was something odd about the new husband. Something that made a shiver go up and down Blythe's spine. The man gave off bad vibes, as her *Englisch* friends would say. She'd dealt with one secretive man. She hoped *Aenti* Rita would be truly happy, but Blythe wanted no part in Rita's new life. Maybe, like her sister, she'd come back to Pinecraft for more than one reason.

Now she just wanted to be at peace.

Blythe hadn't mentioned her concerns about Arthur to anyone, not even Adina. But she'd need to tell Simms. He could take a tidbit of information and track a person's background from the cradle to the grave.

Blythe might be imagining things, but everything she'd thought she'd been imagining had now come to light. Someone wanted to torment her even more, or worse, kill her once and for all.

"I'm made of stronger stuff now," she whispered into the night. "And... I have Simms."

With a gasp, she sat up in bed. "And I'm a widow. Free to remarry." Then she shook her head, the sound of waves hitting the shore matching the beat of her heart. "But I will never marry again."

An image came into her head. An image of

Simms sitting by her hospital bed. As part of his job, as a friend.

That's all she could ever be for him because she couldn't leave her faith and he wouldn't turn back to being Amish. He'd become too hard and cynical and brooding. He hovered over the darkness of life, searching for justice he'd never find.

She'd have to accept that, even if she did notice his fatigue and the deep longing in his eyes. They couldn't become close, but she could be nearby, to watch out for him, to help him, to be a friend to him. To comfort him when he was lonely.

Nothing more, she told herself as she drifted off to sleep.

Nothing more.

She slept, her dreams a messy mixture of running away and turning to find Simms standing there staring at her, that look in his eyes. Eyes that showed her he had a heart. His longing told her he needed grace and love in his life, too.

In the dream, she called out to him.

She woke with a start when she heard a noise outside, behind the house.

Before she could find her cloak, Simms was in her room, grabbing her and dragging her into the den. "Get in the closet and don't come out until I tell you to," he said, his feet bare, his sweatpants old and worn.

Blythe nodded, her heartbeat at full force. "Have they found me already?"

"I don't know. Could be a stray dog or some sort of wild animal. But I'm about to find out."

"Be careful," she whispered as she grabbed a broom from the corner of the closet. She could protect herself if need be.

Then she realized telling someone like Simms to be careful was plain dumb. The man lived for danger.

Blythe sank down, scared but firm on one thing. She couldn't let Simms risk his life for her. She'd been foolish to come to him in the first place.

She'd tell him to move her to a place where no one would know her or find her. She had to keep her family and Simms safe, no matter what happened from here on out.

When she heard gunshots and footsteps, Blythe forgot about staying in the closet. She took the old broom and headed for the back door, her mind full of nightmares and fear, and something new. Anger.

Determined to survive yet again and hopefully, keep Simms alive too, she rushed out into the room when she heard more shots fired. What if they'd brought more people? Blythe feared for Simms. He might be outnumbered.

She couldn't let Simms fight these people

alone. So she held the broom high and stepped out into the dark night, ready to do battle for the one friend she knew she could trust.

THREE

Simms fired another round and heard the rustling of feet in the thick overgrowth just past the beach. Human rustling.

Two men—why did they always come in pairs—who'd been snooping and peeking into windows. Bulletproof windows because he wasn't going to rebuild this house a second time. The locks were solid and the doors were heavy wood. He had smoke detectors in every room. And he had ammo, lots of ammo.

This was becoming tedious. He couldn't tell Blythe the truth when she'd asked him if he ever got tired of this. Yes, he did. But right now he roamed around the trees, darting here and there, listening for more footsteps. When he heard a motor cranking up on the main road, he figured he'd scared them away.

Then he heard a scream that tore through him like a bullet.

Blythe.

Simms hurried toward the cottage and took the front porch with a swift jump. "Blythe?"

He checked the closet and found the door open and no one inside. "She never listens," he said in a growl then followed the wind to the open back door. "Blythe?"

"Here," she called from the beach, her voice lifting in the tropical breeze. "Simms, I'm here."

He ran out onto the white sand, searching in the moonlight until he saw her standing over a body.

"Blythe?"

"He came out of nowhere," she said, her voice calm, her hair flowing in the wind. "I hit him hard with the broom." She held up what was left of his favorite sweeping broom. "It broke."

"I can see that," he replied, taking the jagged handle out of her iron grip. She had a lot of stored-up rage to hit like that. "Let me check on him."

"I might have killed him."

Simms heard the slip of a whimper in that confession. She'd go into shock soon.

He bent down and found the man's throat. "He's still alive, but I imagine he'll have a raging headache." After he'd checked the man for weapons and found a small rope and masking tape in his deep jacket pocket, he used both to bind the man's hands. Then he pulled his phone out of his sweatpants pocket, about to call for help. "How did you even do that?" he asked, trying to keep Blythe from having a meltdown.

Blythe stood still. "I jammed the bristles into his eyes and then I kept hitting him, over and over. I couldn't stop. He lost the knife. The knife." She looked down at her dress. "After he cut me."

Simms whirled and stood. "He injured you?"

She nodded, then she reached for him with her left hand.

She held her right hand over the spot, blood seeping through her clothes and fingers. So near her kidneys. The attacker had missed his aim.

The man lying a few feet away groaned and struggled to stand.

Blythe took one look at her attacker and tried to rush him.

But she stopped, her hands reaching out to Simms. "I don't feel so *gut*, Simms."

He caught her before she hit the sand. After lifting her up, he rushed her inside and then called for backup and an ambulance, while he watched the injured man dragging himself away, his hands still wrapped in tape. He had to keep her alive, but he also wanted the suspect she'd taken down to stay alive. Simms needed answers, but he'd have to let the backup team find the intruder. He couldn't leave Blythe here alone.

Blythe moaned when he laid her on the sofa. "Did I mess up?"

"No, *neh*," he said, his mind all twisted and burning with the urge to do harm to anyone who touched her. "*Neh*, you're going to be fine. Help is coming."

He hurried around, bringing the first aid kit and towels.

"I don't want to kill anyone." She moaned again. "I don't want to be a murderer like Hayden."

"I know. I don't like that either. You are nothing like him." He dug through the kit, found some gauze and held a wad of it to the bleeding cut just underneath her ribs. To keep his mind off how close she'd come to being stabbed to death, and to keep from finishing off the man who'd probably escaped, he said, "Funny thing, and I haven't told anyone this, but I've never killed anyone. I've shot people to stop them, to arrest them. As a rookie, I was trained to hit critical mass—the heart and the forehead. But I have broken that rule. I aim for a leg, to stop them so I can cuff them."

She held her eyes closed. "Simms, you're so sweet."

"I'm not sweet. I just…can't kill another human being."

She reached a hand to his arm, her eyes open

now, bright with shock, pain and realization. "You still have a bit of Amish in you, Simms."

Then she passed out, but he held the gauze against her stomach while he put his other hand over hers.

"I just might at that," he whispered before he said a silent prayer. "If only."

Blythe woke up in the hospital, a scream caught in her throat. *Not back here. Neh.*

She blinked, glanced down and felt the gauze underneath the hospital gown she wore. What had happened?

Her mind whirled between flashes of dreams and the harsh reality that she'd almost died. Again. How many lives did she have left? Not enough. She didn't want to be here either.

Looking around, she saw Simms in a recliner by the window, his eyes closed, his face dark with a five o'clock shadow. She wasn't dreaming. This was real. And this was now, not back then when she'd woken up in the hospital afraid and found the same man waiting to talk to her.

Simms. He was good underneath all that gruff. He'd been through a lot. Things that caused him to walk away from his faith and his people. But he would do anything to help anyone who was Amish. He guarded the Pinecraft community like a superhero protector.

She didn't want to wake him so she lay there and watched him, seeing him at peace for a few moments, his face calm and softened, his breathing regular. He'd saved her yet again. When she thought about last night, she wished things could be different between them. And she wished for certain sure she could live in peace. Would she ever feel safe?

A nurse came in, and Simms jumped up out of his chair like a lion about to attack. "Oh, sorry," he said, his voice gravelly and husky from sleep. He checked out Blythe with a laser-sharp clarity, his gaze moving over her face while his brow furrowed into a deep frown.

"How are you?" he asked, his hands going into his jean pockets for a moment before he jabbed his fingers over his dark, tousled hair. "Did you sleep?"

"I slept. I dreamed. I'm still alive," she said, her own words low and coarse. "I can't believe this is happening all over. It's like a never-ending nightmare."

The nurse gave her a sympathetic glance. "You'll be fine. But another inch or so and… well…you might not be here today."

Simms waited until after the nurse had left, then came to stand near the bed. "I've been looking for a safe place to put you. I heard back early this morning. We found one. We'll be moving you as soon as you're released. They kept you overnight to protect you and let you rest. Your wound was deep, but there was no major damage. The perpetrator who stabbed you got away. You didn't kill him. We've got people looking for him, and I gave the duct tape and the broken broom to the lab to check for DNA on both."

Blythe struggled to keep up. "And *gut* morning to you, too."

"Sorry, it's been a long night," he said, his hands back in his pockets. "A scary night, and I let that man get away."

Because he'd been busy taking care of her. Blythe owed him so much. "You don't scare easily, Simms. Which is why I *do* need to be moved somewhere away from you. I can see that now."

His frown twisted into regret. "Because I almost got you killed?"

"*Neh*, because I won't put you or anyone else in danger. I'm here and last night, you felt obliged to do your job. You could have gone after that man, but you chose to stay with me."

Frustration roared across his face. "Of course I'm doing my job, but this is you, Blythe. It's more than a job. We need to end this thing for good. You can't hide in isolation. We'll protect you—as best we can."

Blythe knew he was right. He'd do the work and he'd do what must be done to keep her alive, but she wouldn't watch him get shot again. Or worse. "Where will I go then?"

"We can talk about that later," he said. "I'm going to speak to the nurses and maybe get some coffee. We have an officer outside, and I'll be right back. Do you need anything? Can I get you a coffee or some hot tea?"

She shook her head. "I'm okay. Will you ask one of the nurses to help me freshen up?"

"Of course. I'll be back in five minutes."

"Take your time," she said. He seemed in a hurry to be done with her, and she couldn't blame him. She had brought trouble back to his territory.

He turned at the door. "Oh, by the way, I called Adina."

"What?" Blythe groaned when she tried to sit up. "I told you I didn't want to involve her."

"She's not involved. I've explained things, and while she's not happy with me, she finally agreed not to come to the hospital. I promised her she'd see you soon. She understands we have to keep you safe for now and that you want her and her family to be safe, too."

Blythe shook her head and groaned. "You know you can't make that kind of promise. I've told you that already."

He stomped back toward her, his snarl like that of a stalking cat. "I made you a promise and

I made Adina a promise. And I'll die trying to make sure I follow through."

"And that is why I must get away. I don't want you to die on my behalf."

"Not your decision." He whirled and left her lying there in shock.

"Grumpy," she said, sarcasm rescuing her from the sinking feeling inside her heart. "I've heard promises made before and none of those worked out."

But she reminded herself, this was Simms. The man could move mountains. Or as he'd said, he'd die trying. When he got back, she'd mentioned *Aenti* Rita's new husband. Simms would be on that like a duck on a June bug. He'd do whatever it took, no matter the danger to himself.

She wouldn't let that happen.

She had no option but to do as he said and let him move her to a place where she'd be safe. And away from him, for his protection. Because someone needed to protect Simms from himself.

Simms scanned every room and corner of the hospital as he hurried back to Blythe's room. He and Nathan had done the same when Nathan's *mamm* had been injured by a criminal and brought here. He did not like a repeat of this case. Whoever was after Blythe had to be connected to her dead husband though, so he couldn't ignore the facts. Meissner's reach was far and wide. He could have set this up, not knowing he'd be dead before his plans came to fruition. But Simms needed solid proof.

He'd studied the reports from the prison up north. The official report said cardiac arrest. A heart attack. Simms figured that was code, and someone had stabbed Meissner in the heart with a shiv. But who? The report showed no evidence of foul play and Meissner had conveniently died away from any video cameras, or someone had messed with the cameras. Another sign that something was amiss. Criminals knew how to hide evidence. He'd have to dig a little deeper and ask more questions. He had a long list of things to do, people to question, files to pull up. Anything that could give him some clues.

His phone buzzed. "Simms," he answered.

"Hey," his captain grunted back. "Your man from last night managed to get himself to a hospital—the one you have the girl in—"

"I'm on it," Simms said, running as he ended the call.

He turned the corner toward Blythe's room, his heart hitting like a mighty sledgehammer against his chest. The officer who'd been at the door wasn't there. Simms slammed the paper cup into a trash can, coffee splattering out into the air, and took off running, adrenaline taking over where the caffeine left off, his mind coming up with all sorts of scenarios as he shoved the door to her room open.

Only to find the bed empty and the bathroom door gaping open. Then he saw blood on the floor and a faint trail leading back to the door and a hallway. Her room wasn't far from an exit door. He headed that way, seeing traces of blood as he moved toward the stairs leading down. Then he saw the officer lying still on one of the landings below, blood soaking his uniform.

Simms took in a breath, closed his eyes and shook his head. He'd walked away for five minutes.

And now Blythe was gone.

FOUR

Simms called out to the nurses to get some help, then reported the status to headquarters as he hurried down the stairs, only stopping to check the downed officer with a quick touch of his fingers. "A pulse. He has a pulse," he shouted to the doctors running toward them. "I'm going after them."

The officer moaned. "Your man...escaped from his room, found her."

Anger slammed through Simms. "The man from last night, yeah I heard. Captain said he was here."

"Yes. He's bleeding. I got in one shot at him."

A dark rage filled Simms. An oversight they'd all have to deal with. The man had been willing to get caught just so he could get in, get to Blythe and get away. With her.

He took the stairs in leaps and came to the exit door leading to a small parking garage. Then he became still and quiet, hugging the cold cement post that concealed him, his mind focused on hearing someone, anyone who moved or breathed.

Holding his breath, he heard something on the other side. A soft moan.

Blythe?

Simms moved like a fleeting shadow around cars and heavy posts, watching the place for movement, his eyes scanning the area. When one of the entrance doors bounced open, he spotted a woman and two children hurrying across the building, the click of their heels on concrete grating against each breath he took. He checked and rechecked, scanning, staring, listening. Just as the woman opened her car door, a cry sounded through the maze of cars. The woman's head came up, surprise in her eyes as she spotted Simms. Then Simms saw them—a man holding Blythe straight across from Simms, forcing her against an open door of a big van with a driver ready at the wheel.

Blythe's gaze landed on Simms and stayed there.

He aimed the gun at the man dressed in hospital scrubs, but the woman and her children were in his line of fire. He couldn't take the shot.

The man saw Blythe staring over his shoulder and whirled.

"Get down," Simms called out. "Get down!"

A shot rang out. The woman screamed and

her little girl started crying. The other child, a boy, watched in fascination, shock making his eyes grow big.

The driver of the van revved the motor. "Get in, man, or I'm leaving."

Simms called to the woman and her children, reaching for his badge. "Sarasota police. Keep the kids down."

The woman ducked between her open car door and another car, holding her confused children close. Simms stayed glued to the outside wall, the open air a wind tunnel, cold and blustery against his skin. Training his gun on the man who held Blythe like a shield, he thought this might be the one time he did the thing he'd tried so hard to avoid.

He had no other choice. In order to save Blythe, he'd have to kill this man.

Before he had time to focus and pull the trigger, Blythe twisted and pivoted back. The man let out a scream of pain and fell away from Blythe. She pushed him hard, causing him to fall into the open door of the van. The jittery driver took off, the old van skidding and hissing as the man floored it, the side door flapping out like an old sheet in the wind, the injured man's leg hanging out and getting hit with each flap. Simms could hear tires squealing and burning as the van exited the building into traffic.

Gone.

Simms registered that as he rushed to Blythe. She stood shaking, a heavy wrench in her hand.

Simms ran, his breath caught in his throat, his blood boiling. He passed the frightened woman and her now-wailing children. "Help is on the way."

Then he reached Blythe and pulled her into his arms. "How did you—?"

"When he opened the door, I saw it inside an old workbag," she said, her words coming as she gulped in air. "After he heard you call out to the others, he got distracted and I was able to grab it before he saw. He's weaker than I am, I think."

Simms looked her over. "But you didn't hit him over the head?"

"*Neh*," she said, tear stains on her face. "I hit him in his stomach."

"You sure have good aim," he whispered, thinking first a broom and now a heavy wrench. Blythe must have learned the hard way how to grab anything to use for a weapon. Pushing her gently against a car next to where they stood, he said, "Stay here. I need to check on that woman and her kids."

She nodded, her complexion pale, her eyes full of fear and shock. "I hope I didn't kill him."

"You didn't," Simms said, thinking he'd have done it if given the shot. "He was moaning and he'll be banged up."

Simms shouted a description of the van to the first responders. "Tan, with a rusty dent on the driver's side door. Headed east toward the bay bridge."

Blythe had once again saved herself.

But he worried that one day this woman, who'd been through so much, would unleash the silent scream inside her head, and he couldn't imagine what might happen then. He only hoped he could spare her more trauma by finding the people who wanted to abduct her.

"Not kill her," he whispered to himself, remembering what she'd told him about the men in the woods saying they needed to tie up some loose ends. And the man who'd stabbed her could have easily gone for her kidney, but he'd aimed away and the cut hadn't been very deep. That meant they needed her alive.

Which could be even more dangerous for Blythe. Because once they had her and got what they wanted, then they'd make sure she was dead.

After Blythe was checked over and released, Simms found a hotel suite where they could stay until he moved Blythe to a location the captain was setting up. He had yet to tell her where they'd be going.

"Captain Walker will meet us here to explain everything. I will make sure you're safe, and when we get you to this next place, you'll have a female plainclothes officer with you at all times."

"Where will you be?" she asked as they drove through the night. Her wound was bandaged tight again after some of the stitches had broken. The hospital staff had cleaned the wound and sutured it. Her doctor suggested she stay overnight again but she and Simms both said no—at the same time.

"Too dangerous," Simms replied. "Their man failed so they'll keep coming."

So here they were driving through the city again, but this time Simms had a heavy-duty unmarked pickup truck that belonged to the police.

"This is how we transport people who are in hiding," he'd explained. "Not so conspicuous since a lot of people drive trucks around here. Mostly the fishermen and the orange growers."

"Whatever works," she replied, sleep and pain pills overtaking her strength. "I wish I could see Adina."

"You'll see her soon," he said. "I'm keeping in touch with Nathan. They will let us know if anyone comes snooping around."

Blythe nodded. "I remember Adina talking about a baseball bat that came in handy when people were after her."

"Well, that's a good weapon, and you seem capable of using it."

She smiled at that. "I grab what I can to protect myself and others."

"Just be careful. Sometimes that can backfire on you."

"You saved me for what, about the fourth time?"

"You won't let me save you. You've done a pretty good job of that on your own."

"But having you nearby helps."

She glanced over at him and saw he'd gone still. Learning his social cues kept her fascinated, even when she was scared. Simms didn't want to talk about being near her, obviously.

"You'd rather not do this, right?"

His glance cut toward her. "What makes you think that?"

"You're always in a hurry to get me to the next place."

"I'm in a hurry to keep you safe, Blythe. Why do you doubt me so much?"

She inhaled a breath, regarding his question carefully because she did trust him. "I'm used to people wanting to get rid of me, Simms. First, my *aenti*, then Hayden and now these people he must have sent before he died. But why? What do I have that they think they need?"

"I know what you have that I need," he retorted, his tone deep and firm.

Shocked, she twisted in the seat. "What would that be?"

"Your life," he retorted. "I want to keep you alive."

"So you like me a little bit, huh?" she said to hide the beating of her heart, the hope in those beats streaming like ribbons against her soul.

"I like you well enough."

She glanced over at him but he kept his eyes on the road. Still. Silent. Stone.

"You don't like talking about personal stuff or your feelings, do you?"

"I thought we were having a good conversation."

She laughed and held tight as he glanced in the rearview mirror and hit the gas. "What's wrong?"

"I think we're being tailed."

She tried to see, but Simms grabbed her arm. "Do not look back. Stay there, face forward."

Blythe wanted to scream. "Couldn't they wait a day or so?"

"They won't give up," he replied. "They don't want to kill you yet, Blythe. They want you alive for some reason, for now."

"And then they'll kill me, right?"

Simms didn't answer. He stayed focused on the road and the car following them.

Then he told her, "Hold on. We're about to zigzag across the county."

Blythe braced herself, a prayer caught in her

raw throat, while he zoomed in and out of traffic. Simms was right. There would come a time when she wouldn't be able to find the right weapon to protect herself. He had become her only weapon.

Simms darted around cars and swerved into lanes, but the dark sedan behind them kept coming. He glanced over at Blythe. She looked pale and frightened, but he saw a resolve in her dark eyes that both impressed and scared him. She'd learned to be tough because she'd had a tough life. Losing her parents at a young age, marrying a sociopath who held her against her will and now dealing with the blowback on that. He'd asked one of his colleagues to check deeper into Meissner's death, but he hadn't heard back.

Did someone kill Meissner because they needed something from him and he refused to give it to them? Or did he put the blame on Blythe and indicate she had information, hidden funds, a treasure chest of assets that they wanted, and then they'd killed him?

Did she inadvertently hear or see something more?

Or could Meissner have put out a hit on her before he died, thinking to get revenge?

So many questions and right now, he didn't have time to find the answers.

Seeing a familiar road up ahead, he made sure he could cross over in traffic to make the right turn. "Hold on, Blythe, I think I can lose them if I make this next exit. It loops back to the main road, but only the locals use this shortcut."

Blythe nodded, one hand on the small bar over the window and the other grasping at her wound. She should be resting, not running from people.

Simms focused on the traffic ahead and made his move, shifting between cars until he reached the lane he needed, then he made the turn quickly, without putting on a blinker. Horns blared at him, but they were off the main road now.

Taking in a breath, he pulled the truck up behind an empty house with a For Sale sign out front, making sure they were hidden if anyone came looking. The night was dark, with just a sliver of an arched moon hanging over the moss-covered trees. Dark clouds hovered with a heaviness all around. Bad weather on the way.

"Did we make it?" Blythe asked in a whisper.

"I think so," he said, relieved. Keeping his eyes on the empty street behind the small white house, he asked, "How do you feel?"

"My wound hurts but it's okay," she said. "My brain is exhausted. I don't like being chased."

"No one does," he said. Then he touched his hand to hers, risking everything in that charge of sizzle that went up his arm and jammed into his heart. "We'll get through this."

"I wish I hadn't involved you," she said in a firm tone, her gaze dancing down to his hand on hers. But she didn't pull away. "I'm tired of criminals and murder and people I trust letting me down. I'm just tired." She looked back down, her dark lashes hiding her eyes. "I wish for one beautiful day, walking on the beach again, finding treasures from the sea. Sand dollars are my favorite. They always tell little stories."

"Don't give up, Blythe," he said, squeezing her hand tight and thinking he'd never look at sand dollars in the same way again. "There is still a lot of good in the world."

Lifting her head, she glimpsed over at him, her dark eyes warm and alluring. "Says the man who fights crime every day."

"If I can still tell you not to give up, it should show you that I'm not giving up."

"But could you give up this life?"

That stopped him cold. She'd asked him that before and he was afraid to figure out the reason. Could he? Would he?

He didn't answer the question because he heard a motor purring. The dark sedan slid along the avenue, creeping like a black snake, searching, slivering and slow.

"Get down," he said, pushing his upper body

over Blythe to protect her while he lifted his head an inch to see if the car had stopped.

The sedan slowed, the motor running, the shine on it winking at the moon. Simms held his breath, knowing they could get shot at in a minute's time.

"Simms," Blythe whispered against his hair. "What's going on?"

When the car turned into the driveway, he let go of her and reached for his weapon. "Don't move."

He waited, watched and heard a car door opening and saw a shadow moving up the short drive. Just when he thought they'd been discovered, the man jumped back into the car and it backed out, turning to go the way it had come.

Something had scared them. When he saw a police cruiser turning into the driveway, Simms breathed a sigh of relief.

He put out a report over the radio and then got out, holding his badge high. "Hey, Bert. It's Simms."

"Simms, man, what are you doing here? A neighbor called thinking there was a prowler."

Simms explained. "Can you follow us to our next location?"

He named the hotel. Bert affirmed and sent out a false alarm so no more patrol cars would show up there. Then he described the car Simms had seen.

Simms was walking back to where Blythe sat in the truck when his phone rang.

"Well, I've got an update," the captain said without preamble. "We found the van in a swampy pond just off the bay road."

"Did you get the suspects?"

"Yep. Got 'em all right. Both floating inside the van, both dead. Bullet wounds right to the chest."

"Sniper?"

"Most likely. A trained sniper. You might check around for any retired military person who turned paid mercenary. The people chasing Blythe Meissner seem to have gone from goof-ups to professionals. Someone wants her bad."

Simms got in the truck and stared at the steering wheel, the wheels in his head spinning while he sat still.

"Is everything okay?" Blythe asked, her voice just above a quiver.

"Everything is okay," he replied, not ready to tell her this gruesome news.

She let out a sigh. "I suppose that's all I can hope for."

When they were back on the road with the cruiser trailing them, Simms turned to Blythe. "You're safe for now."

"For now," she echoed. "But they got away again."

But not for long. Those two men had been executed.

"Someone is operating this harassment," he said. "Meissner is dead, so do you have any guesses who that could be?"

She shook her head then said, "He had connections all over the world, Simms. Maybe I should go into witness protection."

"Only as a last resort," he told her. But that thought had crossed his mind. It would be hard for her to start over alone and afraid, but it would keep her alive. And that was the first priority right now.

FIVE

The next morning, Blythe sat in a chair by the bed of her hotel room, her heart thumping against her chest with a protest that bordered on rebellion. No sleep and small bites of a granola bar for breakfast, and being chased by mean people, made her grumpy and angry at the world. She didn't want to be alone, so she kept telling herself Simms was right next door, even if the door between their rooms was shut. Another plainclothes officer was strolling the hallway. Riley. He'd checked on her and told her they'd be moving her sometime today. They'd gotten a room on the third floor near an exit door in case they needed to leave quickly. The exit door was far in the back and heavily guarded. Now dark clouds threatened to unleash in the heavens and that fit perfectly with her stormy attitude this morning. On the run again, moving again. When would it end?

Could they keep her safe in an isolated, distant place away from the city?

When she heard a knock, she bolted out of the chair, searching for a weapon. Old habits.

"Who's there?"

"It's me," Simms called out. "With Officer Riley."

Blythe rushed to the door and swung it open. "You scared me."

Officer Riley gave her a nod. "Morning, ma'am." Then he turned to stand near the door.

"I'm sorry," Simms said. He looked exhausted, but he also was a welcome sight with his scruffy hair and shadow of a beard. He always wore faded jeans, a dark shirt and heavy boots. He held a dangerous façade.

But he'd brought her *kaffe* and a big Danish roll.

"Is something wrong?" she asked, wishing her life could be normal and ordinary, and also wishing she could have a safe, easy relationship with men.

He handed her the food and said, "We've been cleared to put you with a couple who will watch out for you. They've agreed to help us in return for you and me helping them with their work." He shrugged. "They're Amish and they own a produce farm, mostly orange groves, but other fruits and vegetables, too."

"I don't mind work," she replied, relief washing over her while she sipped the fresh brew.

An Amish family and an orange grove seemed like a *wunderbar gut* idea right now. "That will keep my mind off this mess. But what do you mean by you and me? You're going to work with them, too?"

Simms put his hands in his jeans pockets and gave her an almost apologetic smile. "Yes. Captain thinks I need to guard you twenty-four seven, but I'll need to check in at the station now and then."

"Day and night," she said, the words slipping between them like white linen curtains blowing in a breeze.

Officer Riley spoke quietly into the little black gadget on his shoulder.

"Yes, but with others there," Simms said as if he'd had similar thoughts. "A female officer on the property with you as I told you yesterday. And... I'll be around."

He'd be around. Blythe held to those three words. That was about as close to opening up as Simms would get. Could she trust him to be around, to stick with her, to care about her even and not just do his duty for her? She remembered Rita, and how she'd thought things would be different once Blythe had returned back home, that her surly old *aenti* would be kind and loving— the way Blythe and Adina's sweet *mamm* had been. The pain of that hurt and the always-there grief of losing her parents in a buggy accident caused by a drunk driver clawed at her bruised heart. Would Simms stay around?

She had to trust that he'd see her through this, and that she could handle anything if she must. *Gott*'s will.

"That's fine, Simms," she said, her spine lifting in a tight resolve. She took a bite of the warm roll, but it felt like chalk dust against her throat. "When do we leave?"

"Soon." Simms kept his gaze on her. What was he not telling her?

She decided while they waited to fill him in on her thoughts about *Aenti*'s new husband. Why did her instincts seem to flare like a warning when she thought of that man?

"Simms, I need to tell you—"

"We have to leave, right now," Officer Riley said before she could finish. "I just got word from the guys in the lobby. We've got company."

Simms went into action gathering her things with one hand while he held his gun with the other. "Blythe?"

Knowing the routine, Blythe left her food and drink and grabbed her pack and hurried to the door, Simms behind her but holding onto her arm. "Riley, go to the lobby and cover us until I get her in the vehicle."

Officer Riley went in the opposite direction, while Simms moved her down the stairs, checking each landing before they went any farther.

"Clear," he said into the contraption in his ear. Then he motioned her toward the exit doors. When they heard footsteps above, he shoved her out and then gathered her under his arm.

"Stay close," he whispered. "If I see the need for you to run, then you run and don't look back. But stay with me for now."

Blythe nodded, too numb because of the people harassing them, too shattered by the way he'd said those words, to think beyond each step they took, moving behind shrubbery and bare crape myrtle trees that held little protection. They were halfway to the gray SUV when lightning shot through the sky, followed by the boom of thunder.

The rain came in a flurry of water and wind, the cold shower hitting Blythe's face with all the force of darts. She did have a target on her back, and she felt that with each clash of thunder and each lightning strike that shot out of the clouds. It was early morning, but the dark sky made it seem more like late afternoon, offering a protection that came with its own danger.

Then she heard a different kind of boom.

"Shots fired," Simms called into the radio. "East side. We're going west."

When they heard a car roaring toward them,

Simms gave Blythe a concerned gaze. "Run, Blythe. Now!"

Blythe wanted to stay near him, but he gently shoved her. "Go to the vehicle and get in." She heard the beep from his key fob. "It's unlocked."

He pushed the fob into her hand. "If anything happens, you drive yourself out of here."

"I can't drive."

"You'll learn."

Blythe took off, the rain pouring over her like sheets of ice, forcing haggard breaths. It was brutally cold, even though the temperature was in the sixties, but the coastal winds whipped at her like a blizzard. She slipped as gunshots pinged all around her. She didn't dare glance back. Simms told her to keep running.

Out of breath, she reached the SUV and jumped into the driver's seat. She'd driven a car once when she tried to get away from Hayden. His favorite sports car that he'd kept hidden in an old barn. But he and his men had stopped her before she ever made it to the road leading out of his dense property. He's been angrier about her denting the car than her trying to leave. He'd made sure she knew that.

Shivering, her teeth knocking against each other like wind chimes, she quickly studied the layout of the truck's dashboard.

How did she crank the thing?

Checking the fob, she saw a button and pushed it. A blunt silver thing popped up like a pocket-knife. When she heard more gunshots, she searched the steering wheel and saw a wide slit. Testing the fob, she cried out when it went right into the base of the steering wheel.

So now all she had to do was crank the SUV and drive out of the parking spot. But what happened after that?

The passenger door swung open, causing her to let out a scream.

"Drive," Simms said, his gun aimed behind him. "They're coming for us."

"What?"

"Blythe, crank it and put your foot on the gas. Use the steering wheel as if you're guiding a horse."

Blythe did as he asked, the roar of the motor jarring against the rain and thunder. She put her wet sneaker on the pedal and pushed, causing the big vehicle to jump like a real horse.

"Slow for now," Simms said, his voice weak. "Slow and steady but get us out of this parking lot and then we'll switch."

"Okay," she said, keeping her eyes on the wet road. She eased up and held tight to the big steering wheel, her gaze scanning the rearview mirror and the side mirrors—realizing they were there so she could see behind the vehicle.

When she made a right turn, the vehicle skidded but Simms grabbed the wheel and got her back into her lane. Squinting, he took a deep breath. "Hands on the wheel, Blythe. Drive with your right foot pushed against the pedal and use that same foot to brake. It's to the left, Hit it gently."

"Simms?" She glanced at him as his voice went low and shallow, saw the pale of his skin, saw how he slumped against the seat. "Simms? Are you all right?"

"I'm fine," he said, huffing a breath. "Honore, okay?"

Slinking along at a snail's pace, Blythe gave him another glance. "Honore what, Simms?"

"Avenue," he said.

Then he passed out.

"Honore?"

Simms wouldn't wake up. He lay slumped against the passenger-side door, his face gray with exhaustion and pain.

Blythe thought about getting off the road and calling for help, but he'd told her to get away. And she had no idea how to reach the others. She could call 911.

But what if someone had followed them? Simms would want her to keep moving. She'd look for a place to get him some help.

First, she'd have to find the street he'd mentioned. The name was familiar but usually someone else had been doing the driving if she was in a vehicle. Staying in the right lane of the busy thoroughfare, Blythe prayed she'd find a sign to help her. She knew to stop when the traffic lights were red and go when they were green. She wasn't sure about yellow. So she ignored the drivers who honked and hurried around her, her teeth gritting against each other, her hands white-knuckled on the steering wheel. She studied the dashboard while the lights were red, her mind grasping each knob and button. None of it made sense. Then she remembered one of Hayden's drivers talking about the GPS. Global Positioning System. A map that lit up the screen. She'd been fascinated by that when the *Englisch* driver explained it to her. Hayden didn't like her learning such things, but that was his way of manipulating her. GPS! But how could she figure that out?

"Simms," she said, trying to wake him, afraid he was injured worse than she'd thought. Taking a glance at him, she saw he was still breathing and she noticed a streak of blood matted in his hair near his right temple. Had he been shot or hit by another kind of weapon?

He grunted and managed to wake. Staring over at her, he mumbled something. "Okay… okay…"

"Simms, are you all right? How do I get to Honore Avenue?"

His eyes opened a slit as he glanced around. "Stay straight and turn right. About three miles ahead. Keep going…past Fruitville."

Blythe remembered Fruitville. She used to go there with other women to buy produce. "I think I know where we're going now," she said.

Simms laughed then reached for a button on the dash. A map popped up. "Follow directions."

Blythe saw the screen, saw the tiny spec of what had to be their vehicle moving up the street. "That map guides this thing, right?"

He laughed, then winced. "Yep. Just follow the yellow-brick road."

"A brick road?"

"I'm teasing. Keep going and turn right on Honore then stay on it until you're past Fruitville. Klassen Farms."

"Our place?"

"Yes. Our place." He winced, frowned and tried to sit up, but went back down. "And watch your back?"

Then he passed out again.

Watch her back? Oh, watch to see if someone followed them.

Blythe drove slowly again, searching for the street sign, then she checked all the mirrors but the rain caused them to blur, making it impossible to see any suspicious vehicles. When a dark sedan pulled close behind the truck, she gulped in a breath. But the car zoomed around her and kept going. She slowed and checked all the foggy mirrors again, to make sure the car didn't circle around.

Growing more comfortable with the big machine she was somehow managing to guide, Blythe kept praying, the static of Simms radio reminding her they were still in danger.

She didn't know how to respond, so she let the radio keep talking, hoping someone knew their location. When she finally saw Honore Avenue on the upcoming sign, she let out a sigh of relief and did a little fist pump.

Simms giggled, startling her. "You're proud?"

"Of course," she replied, thankful that he was awake and more alert. "I think I can get us to the farm. I've been by there before when…when I used to go to the produce markets."

"You're so smart," he said, his voice draining again.

Then he closed his eyes again.

Blythe got so caught up in the words he'd just said, she didn't see the car approaching them from behind until it had inched close. She had to make this turn.

"Hang on, Simms," she shouted, her hands

twisting the big steering wheel to make a sharp right.

The small tan car rammed the truck's rear bumper just as she was making the turn, causing the truck to skid in a puddle of water. Blythe lost control, her hands fighting as the vehicle fishtailed back around to face the oncoming car. She hit the brakes, causing another skid before she realized she'd made the turn but the truck had landed close to a small drainage ditch and was blocking the road. The car would hit them. The driver didn't stop. He increased the speed and came screeching toward the truck, headed directly for the door Simms was slumped against.

Blythe screamed and tried to turn the truck left and straighten it again, but it was too late. The front end was stuck in the rush of mud slurping through the open drain. A crash sounded inside her own screams and then the truck twisted and skidded and lifted up into the air.

"Blythe!"

She heard Simms calling her name, but she couldn't see him or find him. Then her world went as dark as the sky, the crunch of metal against metal shearing against the terror inside her head.

"Simms?"

His name sounded in the nightmare of her scream.

SIX

Simms came awake with a shout, his hands gripping the dashboard while he tried to figure out what had just happened.

People. People were after them. Blythe. He'd told her to drive. Where was she?

He groaned and pushed his way past the white mass of air bags only to see the driver's door twisted and gaping open.

But no Blythe. Was she okay? Had they taken her? That thought gave him a shot of adrenaline that fueled his climb out of the damaged truck.

He dropped down to the muddy asphalt and searched, scanning the old oaks and palmetto bushes. "Blythe?"

Then he heard sirens. "Blythe?"

"Over here," she called. "Tree."

He blinked and wiped cold rainwater off his face. The big magnolia stood like a giant umbrella right past the foot-high drainage ditch. She sat facing forward, her body curled against the massive trunk as she held her hands over her folded knees, her clothes soaked, her hair matted against her face and shoulders.

"Blythe, I'm coming."

He started across the remains of the rushing water, each step carrying a heaviness that weighed him down, and climbed up the muddy embankment, then dropped and crawled toward where Blythe sat shivering.

He wiped water away from his eyes. "Are you hurt?"

She shook her head. "Just rattled and bruised. I think my stitches are torn again. They got away, Simms. They rammed us and damaged their car, but they just left it there and got into a big van. Only because the police sirens were wailing."

He sat beside her and dug through his wet pocket for his phone. After telling the captain where they were, he put the phone away and turned back to Blythe. She looked so fragile, he couldn't stop himself. He gathered her into his arms and held her tight. "I'm sorry."

"For what?" Shivers followed her question.

"For forcing you to drive."

"Well, you were in no shape to do so."

"Yeah, got knocked on the head, but I managed to get in a shot before I almost passed out."

"Are you better now? You have a swollen spot." She touched a hand to his forehead, causing his blood to pump faster. "The spot has washed clean."

"At least the rain cleared that up. Adrenaline took care of the rest, for now." Then he held his finger underneath her chin. "How about you? Do you hurt anywhere?"

"Just bruised and so tired," she admitted. "I'm still jittery from driving and then being hit, is all."

"I'm glad you're safe," he said, moving his gaze over her face. "A few scratches." He ran a finger across her porcelain skin. "We made it."

"But the people at the hotel?"

"Scattered. I think I injured one, though. Waiting to hear on that."

Blythe looked to where the truck sat with its big wheels buried in mud and grass against the drainage ditch. "I'm sorry I ruined that truck. I think I could get used to driving one, one day."

She wasn't fragile. Not at all. Here she sat, cold and wet and bruised, making light of the danger, using sarcasm in the same way he did— to protect herself. Her emotional self.

"You didn't ruin anything," he replied. "Those assailants did that."

They'd obviously stolen a mundane car to fool everyone and had a backup van to toss her into. Except the hit, which now was a blessing, had caused too much commotion and a traffic jam. So they'd had to flee. He'd find them.

When two patrolmen approached with several EMTs, Simms got up and flashed his ID, then quickly explained he had to get her to a safe place.

"Let 'em check you over," one of the patrolmen said. "Then you can get on with this."

"Check her," Simms replied. "I'm going to look at the scene, in case I can find something to help me pin these people down."

No one argued with him.

Blythe had refused to go back to the hospital. Now she had put her trust in Simms and his method of protecting her. After she'd been cleared and her stitches had been checked, disinfected and bandaged with a clean swath of gauze, she told Simms and the first responders she wanted to get to the safe house.

Simms agreed, a new sheen of grit in his ever-changing eyes. "I think that's wise for now. But if you run a fever or hurt bad, I'm taking you to a hospital myself."

"I'll be okay," she said, her voice weak but her determination strong. "I want to sleep, Simms. Just sleep."

Simms frowned, put his hands in his jeans

pockets, then finally nodded. "We've got an un-marked car on the way."

He stayed by her while they watched a wrecker take away the damaged vehicles, both of which he'd explained would go to the state crime lab so they could search them for DNA and evidence.

"Probably won't find much after this heavy rain, but hey, anything is possible."

She believed him, trusted him now more than she ever had. He had a slight concussion and told the EMTs he knew the protocol. "Not the first time I've had my head slammed."

Now, well past noon, they were going up a long palm-tree-embossed pebbled lane to Klassen Farm, a major produce farm that sent citrus fruits and other fruits and vegetables out across the country. She spotted the citrus groves on both sides of the lane and let out a sigh. The lush trees were just now producing fruit—oranges and lemons—from what she could tell.

"You okay?" Simms asked, his legs crammed against the front seat of the car. He'd chosen to ride in the back with her.

"I am now," she said. "This is beautiful, especially with the late day sun shining across the trees."

"Yep, it's quite the place. The Klassen family has owned this grove for decades and passed it down through the years. They're Amish, and they're well-respected in both the Amish community and the *Englisch* world."

"But why are they willing to harbor me, Simms?" she asked, fear creeping back like a spider on an orange blossom.

"They help people," he said. He sat silent for a moment then turned to face her. "They mostly help young Amish who come here on their *Rumspringa* and immediately get into trouble when they turn to parties, drinking and drugs. They help get them cleaned up and then they allow them to work to make enough wages to get home." He nodded toward the groves on each side. "We can blend in with the crowd here."

Blythe saw this place in a new light. "Are they successful in helping Amish youths?"

"About eighty percent of the time, yes." He shrugged. "There is always someone who leaves the Amish or falters and gets shunned. Even after they open their home, some of the kids turn on them and steal from them. Cora and Edward do what they can and let God take hold of the rest."

"I'm sure they'll consider me a lost cause."

"You need to know your worth, Blythe. You haven't done anything wrong. You just got caught up with the wrong people."

"Because I wanted things I shouldn't have wanted. That's sinful, is it not?"

"It might have been, but you've confessed and you're being faithful now. So let up on yourself."

She wished she could stand strong in her worth, but Blythe missed her sister and her family, and she'd lost years of her life trying to be someone she wasn't. Even *Aenti* Rita had seen that, and at first her *aenti* had been kind to her after she returned home. Now she was beginning to wonder if her *aenti* had something to do with this situation. The woman yearned for money. Blythe had held that same yearning once, and it had only brought her heartache and nearly gotten her killed. Had *Aenti* Rita been nice to her in hopes of getting to the modest bank account Blythe had managed to salvage when Hayden went to prison?

"Hey, you're gonna be okay," Simms said. "I'll make sure of that."

Blythe sighed and gave him a smile. He truly was a heroic person who wanted to get rid of evil. Where she'd once considered him arrogant and patronizing when he'd questioned her in the hospital after they'd found her and Adina, she now understood he sealed up his feelings like a Mason jar with a tight lid.

"I've still got a lot to make up for," she replied. "My battle is not over, Simms."

He touched her hand. "Neither is mine, Blythe. Neither is mine."

* * *

"Come in, come in."

Blythe took in the big white sprawling house and the lovely tropical gardens with stone walking trails curling around the property, then she glanced at Cora Klassen.

Cora was voluminous and petite, her *kapp* neat, her dark blue dress crisp and her graying hair caught up in a braid that peeked out from underneath. She had sweet gray eyes, kind eyes that didn't seem to judge.

"You must be exhausted," Cora said, her expression showing no sign of distaste over their dirty, damp clothing and their bruises. Grabbing two fluffy green towels and handing them to Blythe and Simms, she said, "Go wash up and treat those cuts with the salve you'll find in the washroom cabinet. After you change into the clothes I left for you, we'll have some refreshments and get you both warm. I'll make us some cinnamon tea and I have butter pecan cookies, with cheese and crackers."

Blythe wanted to cry. The ride there had been tense, with Simms driving again, but watching every vehicle behind them, and her twisting her damp apron against her bruised palms. Being on the run was tiresome. A troubled anxiety grabbed at her each time the car braked or sped up, or whenever she heard a horn blowing.

But this? Normal. This place was normal and beautiful, with no evil surrounding it at all. It was clean and sunny and bright, full of color and the freshness of cut flowers and sugar cookies in the oven, full of love and happiness. She wanted to absorb this moment and remember that not everyone in the world was evil or dangerous.

"I would like that," she managed to murmur, her gaze taking in the broad kitchen and the plain dining table that could hold at least twelve people. Then she noticed the big sitting area that held two sofas and two comfortable recliners and had a bay of windows on one side that had a perfect view of an oval lake.

"This is a beautiful home," she said, her shame shouting around her. "I'm very thankful, but I worry about putting you and your family in danger."

Cora shook her head. "Won't be the first time, honey. We are prepared around here."

Simms lifted his chin, his forehead red and swollen with a cut. "We appreciate your willingness, Cora. I know I can trust you and Edward to help me take care of Blythe."

"We feel it's our duty," Cora explained. "We are blessed and we work hard. We always love having others around, and Blythe, a lot of people come here to retreat, to find peace, to get a second chance at life. You'll be just fine."

She guided Blythe to the washroom and told Simms he could change in the office room. "And both of you take care of your other wounds, too," she said, a trace of something obscure in that suggestion. Her next words confirmed that. "You both need to heal."

Simms gave Blythe a glance that held so many things hidden behind those deep blue eyes, things she would love to know. But first, she'd have to tear down that wall he'd built to guard his heart.

Blythe watched him stalk away, then turned and stared out the small window, the sun warm on her skin as she cleaned her cuts and put a fresh bandage on her stitches. Satisfied with that, she slipped on a light-yellow dress and a white apron. After running her hands through her disheveled hair, she managed to twist it up with a few pins Cora had left, then she covered it with a clean white *kapp*. Her boots cleaned up easy enough, so she put on the socks she'd found by the towels and tied her bootstraps.

When she came back into the living area, she spotted Cora.

Blythe nodded to her. "Let me help you in the kitchen."

Simms sat in the living room while Cora guided Blythe toward the long kitchen, where two sinks and a large refrigerator stood by a massive stove and enough counters to can and preserve food for days.

He glanced up, his eyebrows lifting with appreciation. "You clean up nicely."

"It feels *gut* to be clean," she replied, embarrassed, her heart burning with something she couldn't explain.

"Edward is on his way," Cora explained when Simms looked around in what seemed like desperation. "He and the boys are making sure all the fences are secure."

"Boys?" Blythe hadn't expected children to be involved.

"Our two grown sons, Eddie and Terrance," Cora replied. "I'm working hard to find both of them wives."

She eyed Blythe then glanced at Simms. "But don't worry. I won't push my boys off on you."

She gave Simms another glance, her smile hiding something Blythe found secretive. But right now, she didn't have time to figure out any more secrets. She was a stranger, living a life she knew well, but in a new place, a place so different from what she'd known and seen, she longed to stay here forever. But for her, this was just a façade. Blythe didn't have a real life, the kind she dreamed of, but for now she felt safe. But would this feeling last?

Simms turned to her, interrupting her thoughts

again with those shimmering eyes. "They also have three girls. Mira, who's the oldest, then Amy, who is a twin to Eddie, and Agatha who is six now."

Surprised that he was so familiar with this big family, Blythe reminded herself that while Simms wasn't Amish anymore, she'd always heard he watched over the Amish community in Pinecraft. And beyond it seemed, since this farm was about twenty miles from town.

"I'll be glad to meet all of your children, Cora," she finally said. "I've always wondered what it would be like in a big family."

"You'll soon see," Cora said with a chuckle. "Mira is engaged and will have her wedding here in a few weeks. She teaches our scholars—the children of our workers and some other Amish families that live around us. She takes and brings Agatha home with her," she explained. "And our Amy works in one of our produce markets and is engaged to a fine young man."

"How can I ever remember all of this," Blythe said to hide the tug of pain as memories of her own elaborate wedding moved through her head.

"You'll learn their names and probably more about them than you want to know," Cora said with a big smile.

"I feel safe here," Blythe finally said. "*Denke* for that, Cora."

Then she noticed the way Simms was watching her and got all nervous again. She needed to hide her growing feelings for a man she could never be with. He was here only to protect her, and nothing more. No matter how his dark gaze roamed over her face with a sad reluctance.

Edward came in later, all smiles and asking for some food. Simms liked seeing Blythe so relaxed and happy while she helped with that request then went back to chatting with Cora and Mira. She and Mira were about the same age. Agatha had taken a liking to Blythe, too. They'd giggled and laughed while little Aggie showed Blythe her tiny kitchen tucked away in the corner of the big den.

"My *daed* built this for me," Aggie explained with a snaggle-toothed smile. "I cook here almost every day," she added with a dramatic sigh. "*Mamm* says a woman's work is never done."

Blythe had nodded and laughed, until she'd looked up at Simms. Then she blushed, her high cheekbones making her look regal, and accepted a cup of pretend tea from Aggie.

The sweet scene had embedded itself in his brain and refused to disappear. He'd never have that in his life—a wife and a child laughing together. It was a pretty façade.

Right now would be as happy as she could

get, considering they were on the watch and still in danger. He hated to leave her even for a few hours, but Cora had suggested she stay in the main house tonight. The other house would still be there in the morning.

"Blythe can sleep with me," Mira had offered. "I'll catch you up on how things work around here, Blythe."

"*Denke*," Blythe had replied, clearly glad to be mixed in with this family.

Simms agreed, thinking Blythe would feel more at home in the smaller house by the light of day. A female officer would come out tomorrow. Meanwhile, he had some research to do on background checks and what really happened to Hayden Meissner in that prison cell.

While he watched Edward enjoy his meal, Simms went back over everything percolating in his brain.

Someone with money had hired what seemed like every hit man in Florida to chase Blythe. She could have easily been killed that first night, but they wanted her alive. So they'd keep coming until they could corner her and abduct her again. Next time, once they had what they needed, she'd be dead.

What did they think she had? Money? She claimed she only had a modest account, that she wanted none of Hayden's evil money. Did she

have even more evidence that she didn't realize would bring her harm? They'd cleaned up
Hayden's organization. Or so he'd thought. Had
his department missed something?

Then he thought about her greedy *aenti*. Rita
had pushed Blythe into marrying Hayden, thinking she'd get some of the same good life he was
offering Blythe. When that didn't pan out, Rita
had turned on the sisters and told Hayden exactly
what was happening—that Blythe had evidence
to use against him. He'd taken his wife and then
he'd tried to kill her sister Adina because he
knew Blythe had a flash drive with incriminating information on it.

Thankful that he and Nathan, followed by
half the state's best law officers, had saved them
both, Simms only wanted to do that again for
Blythe. One last case maybe.

He was in his early thirties, but his head and
heart were both getting too old and cynical for
this. For now, he sat with Edward and enjoyed
the refreshments Cora and Mira had provided.
So normal, such a lovely fall Florida sunset, such
a beautiful farm.

But as Simms took Agatha in his arms to wish
her a good night, he accepted that even here, the
nice days might not last.

"What are you thinking?" Edward asked
Simms after he'd found some more lemonade

and a few cookies. The Klassen brothers had skedaddled off to a softball game. The women had headed to other parts of the house to find linens and more clothes for Simms and Blythe. He had to laugh when Aggie had offered Blythe some of her clothes.

"We tend to eat supper in groups. Everyone will soon come rushing through the doors, ready for their turn," Cora had told them earlier. "Best get you two what you'll need to live among us, before I slap forget about all of it."

"Simms? You're way out there in the weeds. What's on your mind?"

Simms chuckled at his friend's questions. He was comfortable with the older Amish man, who knew his background since Simms had confided in Edward long ago after he'd help solve a robbery that had taken place in one of their produce warehouses. Edward was quiet and a good listener, like a father to Simms. His kindness didn't make him weak, however. Edward would do whatever he needed to protect his family or his friends, and he'd do it within the tenets of his faith.

Unlike Simms, who'd left his faith feeling helpless and lost, and determined to rid the world of people like those who had swindled his kind, innocent father.

Thinking of his old life back in Pennsylvania, Simms cleared his throat, aware of the way Edward studied him now. "You're always able to read me."

"I can, but I've never seen you so worked up, so determined. You care for her, ain't so?"

Did that secret flash across his forehead like an electronic road sign, Simms wondered.

"I care about anyone I'm trying to keep alive," he retorted, hoping Edward would buy it.

He didn't. "But not all of them are young and pretty and Amish," Edward pointed out, his salt-and-pepper beard dancing with a quiet rumble of laughter. "This one comes with a notorious background and a bundle of neediness."

"There is that," Simms admitted. "I've known Blythe for a while now. I'm familiar with what she's been through and thought she'd be okay once she went back to Pennsylvania, and yet here we are again." He sighed. "We became close after she survived her husband's criminal activities, but she decided to go back to Campton Creek and start over." When he saw Edward's expression piqued with interest, he added, "We got close, but it was a brief friendship, nothing more."

Edward rocked in his rocking chair, his head nodding along with his chair. "And now she's here again and needing your help."

"Yes, but Edward, she is not that needy. She's

afraid but the woman has taken matters into her own hands. She's too brave and fierce to know better. So it's up to me to keep her safe."

"Yep."

"What does that mean?" Simms asked, shaking his head.

"Yep means you care about her more than you know, my friend."

"I guess I could care if I pushed the issue."

Edward's expression softened. "And yet, it is forbidden."

"*It* meaning her and me being anything but friends?"

"That indeed."

"That is correct," Simms replied. "But I am to go undercover as an Amish man so I can come and go as needed. To protect her."

"And yourself, of course."

Simms rubbed his sore head. "Maybe a hat will help."

Edward laughed, but when they heard the women returning from upstairs, he gave Simms a serious glance. "I will keep you in my prayers, my friend."

"I'd expect nothing less," Simms replied. He'd need all the prayers he could get with this case. And this woman.

SEVEN

The next afternoon, Simms arrived without much more information to report. He breathed a sigh of relief when his officers reported a calm night. Blythe told him she'd slept well in the room with Mira, and today she'd stayed busy in the main house, helping Cora where she was needed.

"And a *gut* thing," Cora added, watching Blythe and Agatha playing house again. "We've been busy all day. But the *grossdaddi haus* is ready. I saw to that personally."

Now with the sun hovering over the western horizon, they'd finished touring the orange groves and the rest of the property while some of Sarasota's best stood guard around the perimeters.

Simms was proud that his police department had eyes on Blythe. They'd worked for years trying to pin something on Hayden Meissner, and they wanted to find any leftover criminals who might be thinking of continuing his devious ways of doing business. If she hadn't come to him for help, the department wouldn't have known something was still bubbling with his cronies and underlings.

"You'll stay in this *haus*," Cora said to Blythe after they'd stopped the four-seater golf cart they used to get around the property by the tiny cottage connected with a dogtrot porch to the main house.

"It's so pretty," she said, her smile full of surprise. "I noticed it yesterday, so I'm glad I'll be near the main *haus*."

"We use it a lot for the youth who come here for help," Edward explained. "Right now, however, we only have a couple of young men, Adam Hammond and Jeff Wilson. They usually room with our sons, mainly because they've been known to act out, so we can't put them out here alone. But they are with one of our drivers who needed help with a large delivery. They'll be back tomorrow."

Simms laughed and shot a glance at Blythe. "As you saw at supper last night, the Klassen lads are strong and forceful. Terrance is the oldest and Eddie, while a twin of Amy, is as strong as an ox. They keep the wild youngies intact."

"And Mira is a spitfire," Edward said, shaking his head. "She'll set the boys straight if need be. But they won't bother you."

"We have informed our children about your situation, but Adam and Jeff won't be aware of the officers we have on watch," Edward told her. "So don't mention that to them."

Cora explained, "We never tell any of our boarders about such things. They'd either get in trouble or run away if they knew the authorities were hovering about."

Blythe lifted her chin. "I understand what I'm to say. We're new hires for the season, and we're friends," she said, repeating what Simms had told her earlier, which was accurate. Especially the being friends part, he reminded himself. And she reminded him, "You'll sleep in the small loft in the barn when you have to stay over, and I'll have a female with me here."

"That's correct," he replied, wishing so many things he couldn't say out loud. "Dana will have a phone and I'll have mine."

Cora touched her hand. "Dana will dress Amish, and you can tell everyone she's your cousin."

"Dana is a big help to us, especially with the young girls we try to take care of," Edward said, shrugging. "She comes from a Mennonite family, but has lost most of her relatives, so she considers us family even if she lives in the *Englisch* world. And if you're here, you're considered family, too, now."

Blythe's onyx-eyed gaze slipped over Simms. "I appreciate that. I hope this will be over soon, but we've been through so much already, I fear it's only the beginning."

"*Gott* will protect us," Edward said. "And He has given us provision to be alert and aware. Farming requires that, as you both know. Growing produce and raising animals is a never-ending feat, and we have our share of poachers and intruders. So we're ever watchful."

"Well, it's been a long day," Cora said. "Tomorrow, Blythe, since it's Saturday, you'll spend some more time with my girls and they'll show you what other work is needed."

"I'll do any kind of work," she said, her tone strong and sure. "I enjoyed staying busy today."

Simms believed her. Blythe wasn't a slacker. She'd just gotten used to the good life, but it hadn't taken her long to fall right back into a plain Amish way of life. He was proud of her for that, but he wasn't sure he'd ever be capable of going back to the plain life himself. Not that he didn't know hard work, but he didn't belong there anymore.

"I'll sit with you until Dana shows up," Simms said to her. "I need to see the layout of the cottage anyway."

Edward gave his wife a knowing nod. "I'm tired, my love. Let's head to our recliners."

"*Gut* idea," Cora replied. "Blythe, if you need anything, remember the walkie-talkie I left in the kitchen." She lifted her hand toward the cottage. "We keep ours right by our bed, so if you can't reach either of your protectors, you can signal us anytime, no matter how late it is."

Glancing at Simms, Cora said, "There's a bag of Amish clothes for you to take with you. Wear them each time you come here, understand?"

"I do," Simms replied. "Done that many times."

"He knows his job," Edward said to Cora with a smile.

"That he does," Cora replied. "But this time, we have to keep to the plan. No going off all bolstered up, Simms."

Simms held both hands up, palms forward. "By the book, Cora. I promise."

Edward bobbed his head. "Amen to that."

Simms shook Edward's hand. "*Denke* again. I appreciate this."

"Always," Edward said. "Just be careful, Simms."

After they walked away, Simms turned to Blythe. "Well, what do you think?"

"They seem to love you, is what I think. They don't shun you for jumping the fence."

"I wasn't really referring to that, but yes, they are kind and thoughtful. I like that they consider me family. What I really want to know is how you feel about being here."

She stood staring across the vast grove, then she let out a content sigh and smiled. The evening sun had left a splash of blue, pink and lavender colors cascading across the sky. "I think this is paradise, but I know evil is just outside those gates."

"For now, we have a reprieve," he replied. "But you're right. These people won't stop. I've got our tech experts trying to track down any connections Hayden may have left behind. Most of his cronies went scattering into the wind, but we tracked as many as we could."

Blythe gave him one of her blunt stares, her dark eyes wide, her frown almost an accepting smile. "You like to do things your way, ain't so?"

"Doesn't everyone?"

"I heard the warnings Cora and Edward gave to you, and I've seen you in action. I agree with them. Be careful."

"I'm always careful, Blythe," he retorted, wondering if she cared enough or was just making sure he'd do his job and protect her. "Besides, you're one to talk. You found incriminating information regarding your husband and almost died trying to make sure that information got in the right hands."

"We do what we have to when things get

messed up," she replied. "I'm so very tired of worrying about the people who are worrying about me."

Simms felt that tug to comfort her, but he wasn't the comforting type. Or he hadn't been. This spry woman had softened his sharp edges, and he wasn't so sure how he felt about that.

"Remember, Blythe," he said in a whisper while they waited on a small porch for Dana to show up. "They might be out there, but I'll be right here nearby. You can count on that."

Blythe didn't respond. She put her hands across her stomach in an age-old stance of protection and stared at the now pink-and-orange afterglow of the setting sun. Simms could see the strength in the way she held her spine straight, and kept her gaze firmly planted on the distant horizon. A fighter, this one.

He only hoped she didn't go off-book herself.

She finally turned to Simms, her eyes glistening like black diamonds in the coming night. "You're about the *only* one I can count on."

Simms didn't like the resolve in her voice, but she was right. They had to depend on each other now, no matter what.

They stood there on the porch, watching the gloaming fall across the fruit trees, the scent of fragrant flowers in the humid air.

Simms thought about how nice this was, to be

here in this small home with a beautiful grove of trees sloping down the hill, and bright tropical hibiscus and oleander trees everywhere. A rare quiet moment that was indeed paradise.

A grating noise coming from inside the house shattered the peaceful evening.

Blythe gasped, but Simms put a finger to her mouth. "Shhh."

Simms pulled out his concealed weapon and pushed the door open. They'd toured the house and left it unlocked while they talked to Cora and Edward in the backyard. Blythe thought they were safe here, but that façade went away with the noise echoing from inside the small cottage.

Another noise—the sound of a dish breaking as it hit the floor in a blast of heavy bumps.

"Stay here," he said. Then he shook his head. "Stay behind me."

Blythe didn't mind him shielding her as he slowly pushed the front door open. Shielding her with his body, Simms called out, "Police. Come out with your hands up."

When they heard a whimper and then a bark, Simms looked at Blythe, relief in his high-alert eyes.

"Bloomer?"

A big yelp, followed by a woof, and a huge dog

with shiny tan fur came running toward them and pounced on Simms.

"Okay, okay. Down boy," Simms said, grinning as the big dog tried to lick his face. "How did you get in here?"

"A dog?" Blythe said, relief flashing through her eyes. "I think I saw this dog earlier, running behind some of the workers."

Setting the dog down, Simms grabbed Blythe's hand. "Bloomer is the resident mascot. He follows everyone around. Let him sniff your knuckles and you'll be his friend for life."

Blythe let out a sigh. "You scared me so badly, my hands are trembling." She did as Simms said and let the mutt sniff her. "I think you probably found that oatmeal bread Cora gave us to have for breakfast. You have crumbs on your whiskers."

Bloomer took that as an invitation to give her doggie kisses, too, which made Blythe start laughing.

Until she looked up and into Simms's eyes. They were a fire-blue, burning with some sort of emotion she couldn't read.

Pushing the lovable dog away, she frowned at Simms. "Are you all right?"

"Uh, yeah," he said. "Just surprised. And I'm guessing the trash container got knocked over while this one was rummaging for his supper."

The moment of flaring heat in his eyes was gone. Blythe watched it slip away with a longing that burned just as deep in her soul. "You seem to know this creature quite well."

"As I said, he's the farm dog—named Bloomer because when he was a puppy he loved chasing the blossoms that fall off the trees around here. He's a harmless mutt—part golden retriever and part hound, we think. He wanders around and can sometimes be gone for hours, but he always shows up for supper."

"But how did he get in?" she asked, fear still pounding against her chest with a drumming pulse—that reminder that even this paradise wasn't safe. "I did see him earlier, but I thought he belonged to some of the workers. This is the first time I've seen him up close. Why was he in the cottage?"

"That I don't know. We did leave the door cracked when we walked back outside earlier."

"I guess he sneaked right by us." She glanced around, taking in the simple, clean, fresh-smelling little house, and the broken plate and bread-crumbs on the floor. The trash can was empty and clean, thankfully. Just toppled on its side. "I like this place, but I doubt I'll ever relax until this is over."

Simms put away his gun, his eyes gleaming

with an apathy that shielded anything else he might be thinking. "I'll get this cleaned up."

Blythe felt the coolness of that gleam. This man was *gut* at shutting down his feelings, whatever they were.

"Bloomer, where are you?"

At the sound of that sweet call, they both turned and went back out the door, Bloomer leading the way. Agatha stood in the yard, the afterglow of the sunset behind her making the scene look like a portrait.

"There you are," she said, clapping her hands at the dog rushing toward her. "*Mamm* said you'd probably come here to meet the new hires."

"Agatha, does your *mamm* know you're out here?" Simms said, lifting the giggling little girl into his arms while Bloomer yelped. "Your dog is in trouble. He broke a dish and ate most of what was to be Blythe's breakfast tomorrow."

"Bloomer, you know better," the charming golden-headed *kinder* said with a wag of her tiny finger while Simms grinned over at her. "Blythe, I will cook you some eggs in my kitchen."

"That's very kind."

It was Blythe's turn to feel a fire inside her, and she was certain sure her eyes were burning in the same way Simms's had been earlier. To see him holding a child did something to her insides that made her think of butter and honey melting on a biscuit. Had he felt that when she'd been laughing with Bloomer?

Were they both so on edge and too alert of danger to be aware of the other thing they'd one day have to deal with?

This attraction between them had blossomed just like an orange tree, and now being forced together had made them both even more aware of the fire that seemed to warm their souls.

Simms gave Blythe a quick smile. "Aggie makes the best egg biscuits. And they have no calories."

"I like that idea," Blythe said, thinking she'd love to have a child like this one. Aggie obviously loved to play house.

"I will let you make me breakfast, for certain sure," Blythe said, glad the dog and the *kinder* were a distraction. A *gut* distraction.

"I'll pretend to buy what I need to prepare." The young girl bobbed her head, causing her curls to bounce while she studied Blythe with an innocent but obvious intent and sized her up with a bluntness that showed her precarious personality.

Then she asked, "Are you Simms's wife?"

Blythe lifted her gaze to Simms, her heart stopping as she blushed. Agatha had not been in on the discussion of why they were here. "*Neh.* He is—we are—"

"Friends," he finished, as flushed as she was sure she looked. "We're here to work with your *daed* and *mamm*."

Agatha studied both of them with her pure green gaze. "Okay," she finally said, leaving whatever she'd been thinking to herself. "I always have to go to bed early, so I miss important information sometimes."

"We should get you back to the house," Simms said, his tone gentle but firm while his expression seemed pasted into place. "Did you slip away?"

"*Mamm* told me to find Bloomer," Agatha said with a missing-tooth grin. "Except I wasn't supposed to come around to the far back of the house."

"Then let me escort you and Bloomer home," Simms said, glancing back at Blythe. "Do you mind if Blythe comes with us?"

"*Neh*," Agatha replied, her dog almost as tall as her. "*Mamm* said Blythe is pretty, and *Mamm* thinks you're sweet on her." She shrugged. "I thought if you're moving into the *grossdaddi haus* you might be like *Mamm* and *Daed*—married."

Simms started coughing and then recovered as he glanced at Blythe. "Well, she is pretty, that's for certain sure. And I—"

Blythe took over. "And he is a *gut* friend who

wishes he didn't have to hang around me all day. Let's get you home."

"Nice save," Simms said with what looked like relief as they hurried to the big house.

But she wondered. Was he sweet on her? Apparently, everyone around him thought that. She didn't see things that way, however. Simms focused on work and his goal to save the world.

Eddie stood on the porch when they came around the corner, his hair wet from cleaning up. "Agatha, what has *Mamm* told you about wandering away when it's getting dark?"

"I had to find Bloomer," the child replied, a tremble at her lips. "Simms had him."

"He had us," Simms clarified. "He'd somehow gotten into the *grossdaddi haus*."

"That dog has a way of breaking into any building," Eddie said, his smile relaxed. "Sorry he bothered you."

"He scared us," Blythe admitted. "But I'm glad to know him."

"He's not a very *gut* watchdog, but he'll protect anyone he knows," Eddie, a tall lanky fellow with dark blonde hair, told her.

"I'll keep that in mind," she replied, glad this was a false alarm. Bloomer obviously had the run of this massive property.

After they handed Agatha and the dog over to Eddie, Simms checked his phone and turned to

Blythe. "Dana's pulling through the gate right now. So soon you can get some rest. And let her check your stab wound. She's familiar with such things since her mother was a midwife."

"Okay," Blythe said, dreading the darkness. "When will you be back?"

"Sometime tomorrow," he said. "I have work to do at the station, searching for any clues."

"Simms," she said, once he'd checked over the house again, "will you look into a man named Arthur Glick?"

Simms's expression hardened into detective mode. "You remembered someone connected to Meissner?"

"*Neh*, I know him from back home," she explained. "He's *Aenti* Rita's new husband, and he gives me the creeps."

Anger flared in Simms's eyes. "And why didn't you mention this sooner? I considered your *aenti*, and now my instincts tell me I was right in thinking she could be in on this."

Blythe flushed with embarrassment. He'd think she'd hid this information on purpose. "I tried a couple of times, but you know, running for my life had to come first."

He had the grace to look sheepish. "Okay, fair enough. Do you think he might have something to do with these attacks?"

"I can't be sure, and I hesitated because my

aenti loves him and he says he can give her a *gut* life. But there is something about him." She shrugged. "He stares too much and that makes *Aenti* jealous."

Simms stood silent, a frown now etched on his face as he took in the information she should have given him earlier. "I'll find out what that something is. You said they were away. Where did they go?"

Blythe shivered as the humidity took on a damp chill. "They were headed to Upstate New York to visit his relatives, and they planned to stay a couple of weeks."

"Uh-huh. Well, I will certainly do what I can to check on his background. And if you remember anything else, jot it down or let me know right away."

"I will," she said, seeing the disappointment in his expression. "I'm sorry I didn't say something sooner, but I don't want to accuse him if he's not involved."

"The facts will tell us that, Blythe." Then he softened his tone. "Any tidbit, anything that's bothering you, can help, okay?"

"Okay." She needed to be honest with him. Simms had always spoken the truth to her.

A small blue car pulled up to the house.

"That's Dana," he said. "I'll introduce you to her and then I'm out of here. I have a lot of tracking to do. And this one will now take top priority."

He turned to greet the officer who stepped out of the unmarked vehicle.

Blythe glanced at the other woman, taking in the jeans and flannel shirt and the worn leather duffel bag. Dana Wilson was attractive, her blonde hair in a messy knot and her blue eyes bright. She shot Simms a big smile, listened to his instructions, then turned to face Blythe.

"I reckon it's just you and me," she said, her voice soft and Southern. "Let's get you inside, and you can catch me up on things."

Blythe readily agreed, not wanting to linger out in the open. She only hoped Dana could keep them both alive.

EIGHT

Dana chattered away while Blythe took in her surroundings and learned each exit, as Simms had told her to. The little house had a front door facing the long driveway, same as the big house. A small porch covered that entryway. The back porch faced the lake to the east and had a bigger porch with two white wicker chairs and a table centered underneath the big windows.

The kitchen was small but workable and held a nice long counter. It opened into a cozy sitting room with comfortable chairs and a small dark blue settee. The bedroom held a single bed and one window, with a small washroom with an outside door next to the window. Three ways to escape.

Blythe checked the open door to the washroom and turned to go back to the kitchen. But Dana shot past her. "This door needs to be locked."

Blythe's heart did a bump while Dana made

sure the chain lock was on the door. "It must have been unlocked when the Klassens brought y'all in here."

Blythe nodded, but she felt shivers moving like spiders up her spine. "I'll make sure it's locked from now on."

"So will I," Dana said, glancing into closets and armoires.

"Smaller houses are easier to guard, though."

Blythe did a stroll right behind Dana, rechecking the doors and windows. After they'd made the rounds at least twice, Dana nodded her approval. "Okay, we're secure for now," she said. "I didn't see anyone suspicious coming onto the property, and I know where our team has officers stationed."

Blythe noticed how dark the world had become. She turned to study the other woman, her mind still on that unlocked door. Dana fidgeted and fluttered like a little sparrow. To calm herself, she asked, "How long have you been a police officer?"

"Four years," Dana said, her smile making her look even prettier. She had a tough confidence underneath that Southern charm. "I started out as a foot patrol, sometimes a bike patrol, working the parks around town, then got promoted to sergeant this year. That just means more paperwork and heavier cases, such as this one."

Seeing the gleam in Dana's eyes, Blythe asked, "Do you like this kind of work?"

Dana chuckled and put her hands on her hips. "I reckon I'd better. I worked hard to make it this far. I also handle petty crimes and work overtime during spring break. You know, even the Amish kids get in trouble for that one long week."

"I remember spring break," Blythe admitted. "I might have acted out a bit during my *Rumspringa*."

Dana checked the windows, drawing the curtains. "Yep, I'm always amazed that the Amish get to cut loose and go wild before they ask for forgiveness and then settle down."

"It's our tradition," Blythe said, surprised that she was now defending what she'd once felt as a restraint. "It gives us the choice between accepting our faith or walking away, and we mostly always make the right choice."

"Simms tried to explain it to me, but then he made a different choice," Dana replied. "He did walk away. Hey, you hungry? I can make us some pancakes or potato soup."

"We had supper," Blythe said, surprised that Dana knew some of Simms's history. Maybe everyone he worked with knew the truth. "But I do love pancakes. Maybe another time?"

"Sure." Dana gave her a solemn glance. "I'll

just make a peanut-butter-and-jelly sandwich. I saw both in the cabinet."

"Please, make yourself at home," Blythe replied. "There should be some fresh-baked oatmeal bread in there." Then she added, "*Denke* for being here, Dana."

Dana found the homemade bread and sighed. "Oh, I love this stuff. And this dark cherry jam *is* the jam."

Blythe laughed at that. "Cora has plenty in her pantry. She showed me all the things she's canned and stored up. And after seeing her family at the supper table, I can understand why she needs a full supply."

"Such a nice family," Dana replied. "I visit their market up the road a lot. Klassen Produce is the best."

After grabbing a small plate from an upper cabinet, she faced Blythe again, her expression a mixture of curiosity and sympathy. "I've read your file, Blythe. You were brave, testifying against your husband."

"Not that brave," Blythe admitted. "I was so scared I could barely speak."

"But you did, and that's what matters," Dana said. "I admire that. So you and me, we can't keep secrets, okay? Don't be scared to share any little thing with me. I'm discreet and I know my job. But we need the nibbles to find the meat of this situation."

Blythe liked Dana Wilson's bluntness and honesty. The officer had obviously picked up on Blythe's reaction to that unlocked door. Deciding to lean on trust, she said, "You know, I had a feeling when we found the family dog, Bloomer, in this house right before you came."

Dana's eyes lit up in the same way Simms's did when he went into finding-information mode. "What kind of feeling?"

"It's probably nothing," Blythe replied, thinking this sounded silly, "but we found Bloomer in here rummaging around, and even though we didn't shut the door to the big porch while we walked out from the house, I don't see how we'd miss a dog that big jumping onto the porch and going through the door. We were a few feet away." She shrugged and shook her head. "Then I saw the unlocked door to the washroom and my mind went there. If someone was in here before we came to the cottage, they might have left by that door. Or maybe I'm just too jittery these days."

"Blythe," Dana said, moving toward her with a knife full of peanut butter in one hand, "go with your instincts. If you felt something, then something was off. What are you thinking?"

Blythe was glad she had someone to talk to

besides Simms. He'd chastise her for not mentioning her feelings, but she was so twisted up
with fear and confusion, she didn't know if these
feelings had merit. Maybe Dana could at least
calm her suspicions.

"I'm thinking someone put that dog in this
house to scare me," she admitted. "Or they could
have been in here, and ran out that door, leaving
it open enough that Bloomer could get through
it."

"Both valid theories," Dana replied as she
added a big pickle she'd pulled out of a jar in
the refrigerator to her plate. "What does Simms
think?"

Blythe lowered her head. "I didn't say anything to Simms. He might have felt the same
way, but if so, he didn't tell me that. Now that
we've locked the washroom door, I'm wondering if they left that way. Agatha came looking
for her dog. What if we hadn't been here and
someone had taken that little girl?"

Dana put the knife holding her peanut butter
across a slice of bread then pulled out her phone
and chewed at her lips while her fingers danced
against the screen, typing away. "Just making a
note," she explained. "You raise some questions
on that, questions that make sense considering
your situation."

"But what can we do about it, if that's what

happened?" Blythe asked, that nagging fear always two steps ahead of her sensibilities.

"We stay aware and alert," Dana replied while she finished putting her sandwich together. "On top of this thing. Which means I'll keep watch all night. Simms can relieve me in the morning, and I'll bring this up with him."

"A long night," Blythe said, wishing this could be over, her silent prayers asking for the Lord's provision. "*Denke*, Dana."

"No need to keep thanking me. It's what I'm here for," the other woman said. "Simms doesn't like a lot of people, Blythe. But I can tell he likes you a ton. He'll get this done, and you'll finally be free of these criminals."

Blythe nodded, unable to speak for a moment. She wondered if she deserved this kind of protection, but she knew *Gott* would provide for her, one way or another. "I hope so," she said. "I really hope so."

But as the night grew darker, her unrest grew stronger.

What would happen next?

While darkness settled over the city, Simms sat at his desk, his mind on what he'd found and his gut telling him there was still a missing link. Hayden Meissner had died of a fatal heart attack, as he'd already heard. No drugs in his system and nothing else showing up in the toxicology report. The man had a bad heart and no one knew about it, apparently. But then, evil could make any heart bad.

And now justice had balanced that out, Simms believed. *Gott*'s will, his people would say. Still, he needed to find the answer to the question of the day. Did Meissner set this up, hoping to punish Blythe for turning on him? Or was someone trying to play both of them?

He had learned one new bit of information. An Amish woman had come to visit Hayden Meissner the day before he died. He was waiting to hear from the prison about the name on the sign-in sheet. Maybe Blythe would know this person. Could it have been Rita?

The first two attackers back in Campton Creek had told her Meissner was dead. But the unfinished business part could cover a whole lot of territory. Had Meissner left behind a secret account, and did someone want access to that money?

Captain Walker strolled by and grunted. "Don't look so frustrated, Simms. You'll get this figured out. Based on your initial report, I think Blythe Meissner knows more than she's telling."

Simms slid a hand through his hair. "As far as I can tell, she's been honest with me."

"You don't say that with much conviction," Walker replied.

He let out a deep breath. "I'm trying to trust her. She's scared and she's alone. Right now, I'm searching for information on her *aenti*. Rita Zook has married a man by the name of Arthur Glick. So far, I can't see anything incriminating against him, but Blythe felt uncomfortable around him. He and the aunt are in Upstate New York, supposedly visiting family. I've got some Amish connections there, so I've put out the word for anyone who knows they're there to contact me."

"Yeah, but the Amish tend to stay out of things like this," Captain Walker reminded him. "They protect their own."

"Not if one of their own is trying to harm a young woman," Simms replied. "I know a lot can happen in any community, but Blythe is well-known and a bit notorious in Lancaster County, and the Amish gossip train runs all the way to New York and back. I'd think people would want to help her, not harm her, after what she went through. On the other hand, she's vulnerable to scams and people believing she's rich because of all the money Meissner gained illegally. That can be a motive for harassing her and trying to abduct her."

"True," Captain Walker said. Then he scratched the silvery shadow of his beard. "Just keep at it, Simms. If she knows she can trust you, she'll tell all. If she doesn't have any information or knowledge, you'll figure it out."

Simms glanced at his notes. "Two men are dead, and now two are missing and probably dead. They've all tried to get to Blythe. Somebody wants her badly enough to hire hit men to silence those who have failed, and if they do get to her, they'll try to get information. If she gives them what they want, they will surely kill her—the final of those loose ends."

"And she has no clue what they might be after?"

"She just last night mentioned this about the new man in her *aenti*'s life," Simms admitted. "That's troubling."

"So she *was* holding back?"

"Yes, but she said it was because we were being attacked from every corner and also because she didn't want to accuse an innocent man. I have to believe her. She and her *aenti* don't always get along, and Blythe admitted Glick gave her a bad feeling. If this man was flirting with Blythe, the *aenti* could be behind all of this—to get rid of Blythe."

"Trying to hurt her own kin? I don't see it," Walker replied. "But then, Meissner was supposed to be an upstanding citizen, and we know how that went."

"Exactly. But look where Blythe is right now.

She came all the way back to Florida, shaken and frightened. Which means Rita would be rid of her. Her aunt hasn't bothered to even check on her, as far as I can tell. Yet, someone followed her here. I don't think they want to kill her. They just want her for something. Blythe can't trust anyone, but she does trust me. I'm going to keep her close and see if she'll open up even more."

"Well, finish up and get back out to that farm," his boss replied in his grumpy way. "Keep me posted." Then he called out, "And, Simms, by the book, okay? The department is on me about a lot of things, the budget being one of them, so don't try anything that requires money—which means you can't destroy too much property, understand? No more going all cowboy on me."

"Yes, sir," Simms replied, worry nagging at him. He'd found it odd that Bloomer had gotten into the *grossdaddi haus*. He knew Blythe had been scared until she saw the big dog, but how had the dog gotten past them? Bloomer would have run toward them and jumped right in on their conversation with Cora and Edward.

Another thought hit his brain, causing him to get up and gather his things. What if someone had been in the cottage earlier and had left in such a rush, they didn't close the door. Could Bloomer have come in a door on the front of the house while Blythe and he had been walking with Cora and Edward at the far side of the backyard?

If someone had been in that house earlier and left one of the other doors open, the dog could have slipped right inside. And the culprit might have left something inside the house—a listening device, or worse, some sort of bomb that would force everyone out—a distraction to allow them to get to Blythe.

Simms's stomach burned with anxiety. He needed to call Dana and alert her and Blythe.

NINE

Blythe and Dana went back over the events of the day, trying to decide if someone had slipped into the *grossdaddi haus* without anyone seeing them. Simms had called, worried about the same thing.

"I know Cora cleaned it herself," Blythe said, remembering how Cora had explained they were always shorthanded and it wasn't that difficult to keep clean. "She said they use it for when family comes to visit, and for married couples who start out working here and then move on."

"But you didn't see anyone lurking around?"

"Not today." Blythe thought back. "We got here in mid-afternoon. A lot of workers came and went, and I don't know all of them yet. I suppose it could have been easy for someone to leave a door unlocked."

"Easy, too, if no one thought to guard the main house and this one. But knowing Simms, he'd probably already cleared both, with the Klassens' permission. He's kind of thorough like that."

Blythe didn't comment on the obvious. She went back to what she remembered after arriving here. "I do know people—employees—were coming and going all day long. But Simms said they'd all been vetted and only the immediate family knows why I'm here."

Dana heard a motor rumbling and hurried to a window. "Looks like Simms is back, and just in time to discuss this situation."

Blythe felt a warm sweep of relief flowing over her, followed by concern. "He'll want to talk about this, but he won't be pleased."

Simms pounded on the door before Dana could get to it. "Simms?"

"Let me in."

"Moody," Dana whispered before she opened the door. "Where's the fire?"

Simms rushed past her, flushed and out of breath. "I need to check for bugs again," he mouthed on less than a whisper, his gaze briefly sweeping over Blythe. "Any noises or weird things going on."

"Do you know something I don't?" Blythe whispered back, watching as he touched every wall, every door and even the muted lamps on each table.

Finally satisfied, he tugged her to the kitchen and motioned for Dana, who did her own sweep for listening gadgets.

"What happened, Simms?" Dana asked, giving Blythe a warning glance. "Your call got us both going back over things."

"I think someone breached this cottage today."

"You mean, because y'all found Bloomer in here?" Dana asked, nodding.

He stepped back and did another visual scan. "Yeah, did you find something already?"

"No, but Blythe and I were talking about the same thing earlier. She felt strange about finding the dog in here."

He whirled to Blythe. "Why didn't you say something?"

"I thought you could tell I was terrified, but it was just a dog," Blythe replied, hurt at the aggravation she saw in his eyes. "I felt like something was off, and about an hour ago, Dana and I noticed the washroom door wasn't locked. It was closed, but not locked."

Dana intervened, this time giving Simms the warning glare. "She told me about her feelings earlier, an uneasiness she couldn't shake. That's all, Simms. We were discussing how to handle this when you came busting in here."

Simms placed his hands on the long counter, shut his eyes and let out a breath. "I'm sorry. I thought back over the day and it didn't feel right to me either. Someone either lured Bloomer in here, or they left a door cracked trying to get away and the dog came in on his own. Bloomer could have seen them and barked, thinking he had a friend to visit. And they just ran away."

"We've been speculating that, too," Dana said, her tone soft. "Blythe figured it out, and she planned to tell you next time you came, but you're here now and we can go over this place with a fine-tooth comb."

Simms opened his mouth to speak and then shook his head. "You're right. Let's get at it."

But Blythe could tell by his expression and how he whirled right past her that he wasn't pleased with her. Had he really expected her to call him back out here when he'd only just left? He wanted her to trust him, but when would he trust her?

Realizing that he still had doubts about her only made Blythe feel worst. And regret that she'd reached out to him.

Dana rolled her eyes and did a spin. "Right behind you, Simms."

He glanced back. "Blythe, stay close to us. Don't leave my sight."

Blythe followed him into the bedroom, determined to keep quiet when she wanted to ask him how he'd feel if at every turn someone expected him to share every little detail when staying alive was the only detail needed. Taking a calming breath, she thought of all he'd done for her, and all he still had to do to end this nightmare. That did involve the details.

He'd been visibly relieved when they'd told him their suspicions. Could Simms have been afraid of what he'd find here?

She watched as he ran his hand over the furniture and the bed, stopping to pick up the walkie-talkie Cora had given her before he moved on.

Dana stepped back and tugged Blythe to the doorway, then whispered, "I told you he likes you a ton. He gets jittery when he can't make things right. And tonight, he's way off the charts. He came here breathing fire because he cares, Blythe. Keep that in mind and tell him every little thing."

Simms glanced over his shoulder but continued searching through dressers and underneath the bed.

Dana kept Blythe close while they stood at the bedroom door. Blythe thought her heart would crack from all the tension and fear she'd tried to hold back. The kind of crawling fear that held a promise of something bad, a foreboding of things to come. She tried to breathe, but the signs of a panic attack could hit at any time.

Focus on Simms. Focus on this minute. You're safe.

Simms opened a tall two-door closet and pushed back the few pieces of clothing Cora had left inside. Taking a penlight out of his jacket pocket, he slanted it toward the back right corner of the armoire, then let out a grunt and grabbed his phone.

Dana took Blythe by the arm to where Simms kneeled in front of the open doors. She stared at the spot where the light shined on a small black box.

"A bomb?" Dana's reaction shouted through the quiet house.

"Yes," he replied, "and not a homemade one with fertilizer. More of a tactical sort. It's military grade, C-4 or Semtex."

Dana didn't even blink. "How much time, Simms?"

"Probably not nearly enough," he said. "No time for the bomb squad. Take Blythe and get out of here, Dana. And wake up Edward. They need to evacuate the main house. Get everyone out now."

"*Neh*," Blythe said. "I won't leave you, Simms."

"Yes, you will," he shouted as his fingers moved over the wires. "Dana, bring me anything that can cut wires. Hurry, and then get out of here."

Dana ran to the kitchen and came back with a toothy pair of scissors and handed them to Simms's outstretched hand. "These should do the trick."

Simms took the heavy scissors without looking back. "Go. Now!"

"On it," Dana said, staring at the blinking red light on the little black box in the cabinet.

Then she tugged at Blythe's arm. "C'mon. Let's go. I'll alert the family and our officers."

"We can't just leave him," Blythe said. "It's wrong."

"It's the way things work," Dana said, her tone stern. "He can't focus if you're looking over his shoulder."

Once she had Blythe away from the house, Dana, still in casual clothing, spoke into the phone she had hidden in her jeans, explaining the situation and asking for backup. "We have about five minutes," she said. "Simms is working on it."

"Five minutes," Blythe whispered after Dana finished her report. Then she looked over at the other woman as they hurried to the side door of the main house. "You were right, Dana. Every little thing matters when it comes to finding criminals. I won't keep anything from Simms from now on." She took in a sobbing breath. "That is, if he lives through this."

"I'm thinking he'll be fine," Dana said as she tugged Blythe away. "He has a lot to live for, I believe."

A sheen of moisture formed down his backbone and a drop of sweat slid over his right eye and dropped onto his damp shirt. Simms tried to ignore both as he concentrated on the different-colored wires surrounding the explosive package. He had to pick one.

But which one?

His phone vibrated against the wooden floor. Grabbing it, he told the bomb squad expert what he was looking at.

"It's small, but I'm guessing it has enough C-4 to do harm."

"Well, then," his friend said with all the calm of a deep sea, "let's get this done. Just listen to me, Simms. We're on the way, but meantime—"

He didn't have to finish. Simms needed to do his best to stop this.

The detonator was almost as small as a watch face and the solid explosive pack wasn't much bigger than a palm-sized pouch, which meant the power of the bomb wouldn't go far. Just far enough to distract anyone and force Blythe out of the house in the middle of the night. But it could do damage and hurt those nearby.

If Blythe had gone to bed…

After he'd described things and the bomb tech talked him through, Simms saw the seconds slipping away.

He blinked, prayed.

"Are you up to this?" the officer asked. "You can do this, Simms."

Less than two minutes to decide. But there

was only one right thing to do. The fire could spread, and having dozens of first responders here would only add to the chaos. Dana would have alerted the officers already guarding this whole place, and she'd also call for backup beyond the bomb squad.

Simms had no time to wait. "I'm on it."

If he picked the wrong wire, one man down possibly. Him.

Dana knew to get the others to safety.

Simms found it ironic that for once in his life, he was completely and helplessly relying on God. "I can't do this alone," he whispered while his silent prayers rolled by in his head like a scroll on a computer screen.

"Here goes nothing," he whispered. Then he put the heavy black and silver scissors against the red wire his friend had assured him was the right one, with the soft ticking of the bomb following his every move.

Saying one last prayer, he closed the scissors, held his breath and snipped the connection.

Outside, the family gathered around at a safe distance away, with Blythe and Dana. Cora held her husband close, and their sons and daughters were behind them, Eddie holding tight to Agatha. They'd put Bloomer in the barn to keep him out of trouble, and Blythe could hear the big dog barking in frustration.

Blythe held her breath, every prayer centered on Simms. She wanted him to stay alive, and she especially wanted this kind family to stay alive. Couldn't she have had one night of peace?

Cora touched her arm. "Are you all right, Blythe?"

She shook her head, unable to speak. Cora put her arm across Blythe's back and tugged her close. "He's a *gut* man."

"He might die because of me," she managed to whisper, tears forming in her eyes. "I've tried to live the right way, but everything has gone wrong again."

"If he dies, it's because of evil, *liebling*. He wouldn't be in there right now if he didn't believe in what he does."

But did he believe in her or the Lord enough to lean on someone else for a change, Blythe wondered. Could Simms ever get past his doubts? Or would he die to prove his need to find some sort of justice?

Dana checked her watch and gave another update into her phone. Blythe knew there were officers everywhere and the bomb squad was on its way. But would it be too late?

Dana walked over to Blythe, her expression tight and unreadable.

"How long?" Blythe asked. "Tell me."

Dana hesitated and let out a sigh. "Thirty seconds."

Blythe didn't want to count the seconds. She wanted to wake up and find out this was all a bad dream. But the time ticked by and she held a hand to her heart, each beat matching each second. She held her panic back, gritting her teeth and reminding herself of her surroundings, of the people putting their lives on the line for her.

"I'm going in," Dana finally said, her own anxiety tearing through that neutral control she'd held so tight.

"Wait," Edward said, calling out. "Wait."

Then they saw a shadowy figure hurrying across the yard.

"Simms," Blythe said out loud. "Simms," she repeated, her whole body going slack with relief. "Simms."

He walked up to the waiting crowd, his eyes burning like fire, his breath rushing. "I stopped it."

"Obviously," Dana said, her tone full of emotion. "And nearly scared us into a heart attack."

"Did the same with myself," he said, his gaze on Blythe. "I had a squad member guiding me, and we picked the right wire to cut. It wasn't a massive bomb but it was a professional job. In and out, undetected, and the thing was so small you wouldn't have noticed it at first glance."

"*Denke*," Edward said. "You saved our home and our lives."

"It could have been bad," Simms admitted. "Bad enough to mess up your schedules and cause chaos, but we've avoided that and the bomb squad is heading this way to go over everything."

Dana lifted her chin. "If this was a professional job, Simms, then who are we really dealing with here? Certainly not a haphazard crew trying to harass a young woman."

"More than that," he admitted. "Someone is putting out a lot of energy and funding to find you, Blythe."

"And they have," she said. "Where can I go next?"

Edward stepped forward. "You don't go," he said. "You stay here, where someone can always be with you and where we will all keep an eye open for intruders. You don't need to keep running, Blythe."

"I can't stay here either," she replied, shaking her head. "It's not right, getting you involved in my problems."

"We're already involved," Cora said, taking Blythe's hand. "We know the danger, but you need more than protection, Blythe. You need people who will help you and show no judgment. You need to know you're safe." She put a hand on Blythe's heart. "Here."

Blythe looked from Edward to Simms. "What do you think?"

"I think Edward and Cora are right, but we need to make our tormentors think you've moved on. This was an attempt to flush us out, but if we stay it could very well throw them off. Because this little trick didn't work."

"How will we make this work?" Blythe asked. "Do I leave and come back?"

"No," Dana said. "*I'll* leave and sneak back, then put on a wig and dress like you, and Simms and I will leave together, and we'll make a big production—escorts and such."

"And if they keep trying?" Blythe asked, her bones weary.

"We keep pushing back," Simms replied. "I'll help Dana with the decoy, then I'll return to stay here night and day as I promised you. If they come back, we'll make sure they know we mean business. I won't be leaving the property again."

Simms, here night and day. Could she deal with that?

She'd have to because out there in the city, he'd been vulnerable, too. She could watch after him while he watched after her.

Still… She turned to Cora. "Are you sure?

They somehow got into that house in broad daylight. I don't want to leave, but they won't stop until they have me. It's a huge risk."

Cora glanced at her husband and her grown children. "I believe we've decided Edward is right and he is the head of this household. *Gott* will take care of the rest, just as He did tonight."

"*Ech, vell,* the Lord will be busy taking care of all of us," Edward said on a chuckle.

Blythe would do a lot of praying, that was for certain sure. Because even with this danger lurking, she loved this family already. And she didn't want to leave them just yet.

The sirens and a swarm of police cars soon had the place surrounded. Cora corralled her family and Blythe into the main house, while Dana helped the crime scene team.

Blythe sat by the window in the big living area, watching the flashing lights and the first responders, her mind about to explode with dread and anger, her anxiety boiling over.

She'd married a monster, and he'd sent monsters to destroy her. How long could she hold out?

Mira had gone upstairs to settle Agatha down again. She returned and came over and offered Blythe some tea. "Blythe, don't look so worried. We're used to a lot of commotion around here."

Blythe took the tea, but held the cup in her hand, the warmth giving her some comfort. Mira hadn't talked to her too much since they'd both been busy. Shy and quiet, the other woman's gaze wandered over her now, quizzical and curious.

"Chaos and commotions seem to follow me these days," Blythe finally said, watching for a shocked reaction.

Mira smiled. "I have to make a confession. When *Mamm* and *Daed* told me who'd be coming here, I almost fell out of my chair. You're well-known, and I don't mean that in a bad way. You did a *gut* thing, Blythe. You brought down an empire." Mira placed her hand on Blythe's shoulder. "I couldn't wait to meet someone my age, and someone who seems so worldly, but then last night I didn't pester you. I wanted to respect your privacy and let you get some rest."

Blythe shook her head. "I'm touched but you might want to steer clear of me. Worldly is a dangerous path to be on, and I found that out the hard way."

"*Neh*, we can all use a friend and you look like you need one," Mira replied, her gray eyes showing a spark of earnestness. "I'm here and you're here. We're about the same age, and I'm not just trying to butter up to you. It would be nice to have a friend." Her sincere expression showed no hostility. "I want to get to know the real you, not the one everyone has an opinion about."

"I believe you," Blythe said, her heart soaring with hope. "It's *gut* of you and *ja*, I could use a friend." She leaned close. "I had another friend once who betrayed me. An Amish friend who is far away now." She gasped and put a hand to her mouth while a chill went down her spine. "I should have Simms check on her, at that."

The kitchen door opened, and Simms came in and headed straight toward her.

Mira's surprise turned calm. "I need to get back to the kitchen. We'll talk tomorrow," she told Blythe. "Amy is with Agatha, but Aggie was asking about you. We told her you would see her in the morning."

"I'll make a point to visit with her."

Simms thanked Mira then waited a beat before speaking, his steely eyes shadowed with fatigue and concern. "How are you?"

"How do you think?" she said so loudly, Cora and Mira glanced up from where they stood in the kitchen.

"I get it," he said. "This is not easy."

"*Neh*, it's not and if I'd voiced my fears to you earlier, we could have found that bomb sooner. That was too close, Simms."

"I should have done the same and I should

have stayed here," he replied, empathy in his eyes. "I had a bad feeling about finding Bloomer. I'm usually on top of things like that."

"But not with me hanging like an albatross around your neck. I'm a distraction."

Something flickered like a lightning flash in his eyes. "You're not that, Blythe. You need help, and I'm willing to give you that help."

He was covering. That flicker could only mean she had brought him too much trouble and he was trying to soothe her fears.

Giving him her own flicker of fear merging with stubbornness, she asked, "Even if it puts you in constant danger? You know we might not win, right?"

"I know *they* haven't won." He gazed at her with a sweet intensity in those dark ocean-colored eyes. An intensity that wiped away her questions. "I believe I can catch them, sooner or later."

Yet doubt clawed at her like a rabid animal. "And I believe they will win, sooner or later."

"No, I won't let that happen." He leaned in, the gleam in his eyes for her only. "So far, we've managed to keep them at bay."

"But the time will come when they get the upper hand, and I fear for all of us when that happens. If these people are from Hayden's leftover security team, they know everything and

they know how to work around a police department."

"I know how to work around criminals," he
retorted. "Trust? Remember?"

"I'm running out of hope and trust," she admitted. "I need someone to trust *me* right now.
I'm so tired. So very tired."

He lifted her up, his hands strong on her
wrists. "Well, for now, for the rest of the night,
you will rest. Dana and I will take watch. They
won't be back tonight. Too hot with cops around
here."

"And the next time they show up?"

"They'll have me greeting them at the door."

Blythe followed him toward the kitchen and
noticed the curiosity in Cora's eyes.

Simms kept moving. "I'm taking her to rest.
The cottage is clear now and as soon as Dana
goes over some things with our guards, she'll be
in the house with Blythe, dressed as an Amish.
No more bombs and no bugs. If they come back,
they'll have to get past me."

Blythe gave Cora a knowing glance, but Cora
lifted her chin in a subtle nod. Cora believed in
trusting Simms. Mira stood still, her gaze lifting
to Blythe. Again with no condemnation.

Blythe would have to trust all of them. She'd
reached her limit, but she'd keep fighting. For
the sake of this family and for Simms. Hav-

ing declared that, she walked out the door with Simms and then looked over at him once they were alone on the porch of the small cottage.

"We should check to see where Clara is, too, Simms."

TEN

"Clara Kemp." It wasn't a question.

Simms took her into the house and checked over the rooms while he wondered how many more surprises Blythe would reveal. Clara Kemp had befriended Blythe and done the same with Adina when she'd come looking for Blythe. But the young woman had been working with Hayden Meissner the whole time hoping, once Blythe was dead, she'd become Hayden's new wife. He'd pushed her aside, however, once things blew up and they were caught. She was now in prison.

Returning to the small sitting room where she stood near a hanging quilt done in orange and green starburst panels, he asked, "Have you heard from Clara?"

"*Neh*, but I'm doing as you said, mentioning anyone who comes to mind. I considered how she and Hayden might be keeping in touch through letters or messages."

"That's my girl," he said, only to realize by the way her eyes glistened with shock, he shouldn't have said that. "I mean, good job, thinking of her. Wish I'd done the same. I'll check with the warden at the prison in the Panhandle. She's got at least five more years to serve, and that's with time spent in jail here during the trial and with good behavior."

"You understand why I'd be nervous about Clara doing something from behind bars, ain't so?"

"I certainly do, but she'd be wise to walk the line. Prison is no fun, and she is all the way across the state. It's a stretch."

Blythe's expression slipped away like a dying blossom. "I have concluded that I must check on anyone involved with Hayden, as you suggested. Clara came to mind when Mira and I were talking earlier. I told Mira after she said she wanted to be my friend that I had a friend who betrayed me."

"You mentioned Clara?"

"Not by name. I think Mira was being sincere, and yet—"

"And yet, you still have qualms."

"I do, as you well know. My best friend was in love with my husband, and he played that up to get her on his side. Clara truly believed he would marry her once I was out of the way.

Dead. My friend was only biding her time until I was dead. She was my tormentor when they held me in that shack in the swamp. Is it any wonder I don't have or want any friends?"

Simms tempered his frustrations. Blythe had come to him over anyone else for help, so that meant a lot, and that had taken a big amount of courage. "You've been through a trauma that most wouldn't survive. You have a right to hold your thoughts and feelings and keep your secrets close."

Walking up to her, he held his distance but gave her a direct stare. "Sharing anything with me can help us. I won't reveal what you tell me, only the facts and only to my captain and other officers, so we can piece things together." He glanced at the quilt. "Like this pretty thing that someone figured out."

"It is lovely," Blythe replied. "I fell for this house and felt at peace for a few hours, and now I'm afraid again."

"Look, we've cleared it. And I had the tech team put in a quick security system. We put a solar-powered light Edward uses for the barn here near the house. If anyone walks too close, the light shines on them. And it's bright."

Blythe let that settle, then tugged at her apron. "Someone got in here today. Does that mean they were hiding on the property because they knew where we were headed? Or does that mean they were already here working?"

"I can't see any of the workers being involved," Simms admitted. "We talked to most of the ones who live on the property. I have to believe someone is watching us and followed us here, then managed to blend in and get to this house. I'm telling you, Blythe, that won't happen again."

He stood there wanting to hold her. But he'd drawn a line against that. Never get involved with someone you're trying to keep alive. Only he was involved with her. She'd been in his head since the day they'd rescued her, then during the gruesome trial, and now, tonight, she was deeply embedded in his soul.

But she didn't believe he could help her. "Blythe?"

She looked up at him, her long, dark lashes like the wings of a butterfly. She was a butterfly, fluttering from place to place, trying to survive against the wind.

"Blythe?" He held his hands in two tight fists to keep to his pledge. If he made a move, she'd fly away.

"I'm okay, Simms," she finally said, her face a beautiful cameo of fragility pushing against determination. "I'm going to be okay. I know you'll do your best. I only hope the cost of doing your job won't be too high."

Simms didn't care about the job. The cost would be in giving his hard, dried-up heart to a woman who had never known what real love was all about. The cost would be in having to let her go, because he was no longer a part of her world. The world of his long-lost faith. All he could do was watch her as she turned toward the other room and quietly shut the door. And he'd have to do that same thing when this was over and she'd be gone for good.

Over the next few days, Simms helped Edward with work, taking on jobs that allowed him to stay near the main house and the barn just yards away. In between doing chores, he used his phone and connections to find any clues about who might be targeting Blythe. Rita and Arthur Glick were nowhere to be found. No one in New York had seen them. Not family, not friends. Had someone killed them?

He'd have to tell Blythe they were still missing.

He'd stayed close to the house, tending the animals and helping load produce as needed, but he'd tried to avoid talking to Blythe too much. He had to fight this need to be near her, and it had begun to wear on his moods.

Dana followed Blythe and Cora around, helped them with canning and cooking, a hidden weapon underneath her apron, and returned to the cottage before sundown. They also had two plainclothes patrolmen watching the cottage. Agatha stayed near Blythe, too. The young girl had taken a liking to Blythe, so they were now fast friends. Blythe's eyes lit up each time she spotted Aggie running toward her.

That scene of them together stayed with him like a faded postcard. He wanted to reach out and touch those memories but common sense jolted him back.

Now he'd just finished feeding the horses and goats Edward kept on the property mostly to entertain and encourage his children so they'd learn responsibilities, but the animals had their purposes beyond that. Simms had to admit, being back in Amish country even if he no longer lived that life, had brought him a small measure of peace.

Seeing Blythe so happy made him ache for something he'd long ago put out of his mind. Home.

When he saw Dana approaching as he came around the barn, he searched for Blythe. "Where is she?"

"With Cora in the little house," Dana said, her dark blonde hair tidy beneath a *kapp*. "I only hurried out here because I have an update on Clara Kemp."

"Let's hear it," he said, turmoil boiling up and roiling along his stomach.

"She's still behind bars, so we can rule out an escape. She has little correspondence, and what she does have is monitored. Nothing from the now-deceased Hayden Meissner. But…and this is interesting, she has received some letters from Rita Glick."

"Rita Glick?" Simms took off his straw hat and knocked his hair back. "Blythe's aunt?"

"That's the one. The last letter from her was about two weeks ago, according to my source. I didn't mention this to Blythe."

"No, and don't. She's doing better since we haven't had any more incidents this week."

Dana lowered her voice and glanced around. "She's a hard worker, but she's on edge. This would make that worse."

"Why would her *aenti* be sending letters to Clara Kemp?"

"That's just one of many questions," Dana replied. "Have you heard anything from the techs on the DNA or fingerprints from the abandoned car or the bomb from the little house?"

"No. Slow as molasses, as we both know. The bomb squad checked over the bomb before they destroyed it, so they could have found some component to help us." He glanced toward the cottage when the back door opened and Cora came out with Blythe behind her. "I did get an initial report on the bomb, however. As we thought, it's military grade. C-4, but a small amount. Easy to use, of course. And it might have a traceable signature of some kind to identify where it was made."

"That also means someone in this hunt could be military or a veteran, right?"

"Exactly. Or a professional bomb maker—a criminal. I'm going to do some searches on Meissner's 'friend' list and see what pops up. We know Arthur Glick can't be military, but he could know someone who is."

"Did you mention Arthur Glick?" Blythe asked when she came closer. "Have you heard something about my *aenti*?"

Dana backed around to give them some space.

Simms took Blythe and sat with her on the steps. "We checked on the Kemp girl. She's still in prison but…she's been getting letters from your aunt Rita."

Blythe shot down the steps and turned to face him, her teeth clenching, her skin going pale. "What?"

"That's all we know," he said, standing to steady her pacing. He shouldn't have blurted that out, but she did need to know. "It could mean something, or maybe she's just curious about what Clara knew."

"She has no reason, no reason at all to have

any type of correspondence with Clara Kemp. None at all."

"I know that," he said. "We'll find out what's up with that." Then he said the obvious. "Your aunt hasn't tried to get in touch to see if you're in Pinecraft. I talked to Adina to see if she'd heard from Rita. She hasn't, and she sends you a lot of love."

"I miss Adina so much, but I want to keep her safe. Thank you for checking with her. I left word at the General Store that I had an emergency and had to leave for a while, but I saw no need to get in touch with my *aenti*. She isn't worried about anyone but herself."

"If she's sending letters to one of the people who tormented you, then she's not worth being anyone's aunt."

Blythe stared off into the orange grove then flipped around. "What if she was trying to get information from Clara? About Hayden's wealth? She always wondered if he had hidden money somewhere, but I shut her down when I showed her the few thousand dollars I squirreled away when he thought I was using it to buy myself pretty things."

"Do you think your aunt would do that? Try to get to his money or yours?"

Blythe shook her head. "I explained to her about my account. I wanted to keep it there and only use it in emergencies. She suggested I put her name on it, but I refused. Then she met Arthur Glick at a gathering and that took her mind off me and my meager account."

"But she could have questioned Clara," Simms said, jotting notes. "I'll get someone in the Panhandle Sheriff's Department to question Clara. She might have some information."

"Clara won't talk. She hates me."

"She might open up if it can shave some time off her sentence."

"She should stay right where she is."

"Blythe, she can't hurt you."

"I'm not worried about her hurting me, but I am concerned that Rita, who seemed to have changed after Adina and I almost died, is still up to her old tricks. That she might have betrayed me again, and with the evil people who held me to keep me quiet. How many more people are out there, Simms, determined to get to me?"

"I don't know," he said. "But I do know I won't stop until I find every one of them."

Blythe walked off toward the corral fence, her arms held tightly to her stomach as she stared off into the distance.

"That is one troubled young woman," Dana said from behind him. "She's trying to hold things together, but Simms, she could snap and wind up worse off than she is right now."

"I know," he replied. "She had a few months of peace back home and now this."

He needed to go to Blythe and get her into the house. She was too exposed standing there by the fence. "I'll be right back," he told Dana. "Secure the house and let's get her inside until we take supper at the main house."

Dana nodded and he turned back, something off in the trees catching his gaze. A flash of light and then—

"Blythe!" He heard the shot before it hissed through the air. Dana turned from the porch and ran toward where Blythe was standing, a look of surprise and fear clouding her face as she pivoted toward Simms.

"Get down," Simms called to Blythe.

Fear caused her to glance toward the woods. Another shot echoed through the air. Blythe slumped and fell into the grass.

"Blythe?"

Dana hurried to her, but she ducked and lay flat when another shot sizzled through the air.

Simms ran in a crouch, his gun out. Another shot fired just as he reached Blythe and fell in front of her, his body covering hers as he shot back into the trees.

"Blythe?"

She didn't answer.

ELEVEN

Blythe woke with a start and gasped when she saw Simms lying there next to her. "What happened?"

"Are you hurt?" Simms asked, lifting up a few inches so he could see her face.

"No, I think… I think I fainted. Everything went black." She tried to sit up but he pushed her back.

Terror filled her with a panic that cut her breath off. "Let me go."

"Not yet. Active shooter in the woods."

Simms went into full lawman mode, which brought her out of her fears. He'd thrown himself over her to protect her, not hold her down. She was only having a flashback from her former life.

"Dana?" he commanded.

"I'm okay, Simms. Y'all need help?"

"No. They missed." Simms rolled over like a crouching lion and wedged himself between

Blythe and the fence. "Alert the guards and see if they can catch anyone in the woods just west of the front gate."

"On it," Dana called as she lifted up and sat with her legs crossed on the grass, her pink Amish dress draped over her sturdy sneakers, her phone in her hand.

People came running from all directions, calling out and asking questions.

"Get back," Dana called. "It's not safe right now."

Cora saw Dana and shouted. "Is everyone okay?"

"Yes." Dana waved them all away. "We are. Now go back inside." She repeated, "We had an active shooter in the woods."

Cora stared over the wide-open spaces that included the orange groves and the vegetable and fruit crops. "Could be poachers. They're always trying to steal from our farm. We figure they need the food or the money if they sell our produce."

"Have they ever shot at anyone before?" Simms called out.

"*Neh*," Cora said. "What happens now?"

"Go inside Blythe's cottage," Simms said. "When will Mira and Agatha be home?"

"A couple of hours," Cora said. "Edward should be back soon, too."

"Okay, we'll let our men know to check on them and watch for them."

Cora nodded to Simms, then motioned to Blythe. "Come, *liebling*. Let's get you inside."

Simms held Blythe's arm and helped her up. "Stay in front of me, understand."

"*Ja*." She glanced up at him, her disorientation leaving. "They could shoot you."

"They're long gone by now," he replied. "If they'd wanted us dead, we wouldn't be having this conversation."

"So they're still toying with me?"

"Yes," he said as he guided her toward Cora. "And getting bolder in doing so. First that bomb—which could have hurt you if you'd been in that bedroom, but most likely it would have forced you out of the house, and now this, days later. Hired snipers would shoot to kill. These people were just playing with guns."

"Playing with my sanity, too," she said. "I hyperventilated and passed out."

As they met up with Cora and Dana, Simms got her onto the porch then asked, "How long have you been having panic attacks, Blythe?"

Cora and Dana both gave her a sympathetic glance. "Is this true?" Cora asked. "Have you had this happen before?"

"A few, but they were better lately. They

started…after I realized Hayden was lying to me, and they got worst when—"

"When he held you in the swamp," Simms finished, disgust boiling over in his eyes. "You had one just now when the shooting started?"

"I don't know," she admitted. "I was so scared, I froze and then I couldn't breathe. The next thing I knew, I woke up and you were there with me."

"You were only out for a moment," he said, his eyes bright with worry and aggravation. "If I hadn't been able to get to you…"

"You kept your promise, Simms. You told me you'd be here next time they came, and you were."

Simms held his gaze on her, the silence between them sizzling like dry lightning. "And I'll be here next time, but Dana, we need to have a serious talk with the guards posted around here. Someone messed up."

"Don't be so hard on your coworkers," Cora said. "The woods around here are dense and swampy." She gave Blythe an understanding look. "And part of our property isn't fenced, so I can see someone hiding out. I can also understand someone in fear of ever walking into a Florida forest again, too."

Blythe gave each of the three people surrounding her what she hoped was a bold glance. "So even though I'm here in this compound with heavy security, and all of you watching after me, these people have still managed to find me. Why is that? Can anyone explain how they keep finding me?"

"She has a point," Edward told Simms after they'd had a cold supper of sliced vegetables, fresh bread and cheese and pound cake. "We've never had this much antagonism and believe me, we've had all kinds of troubled teenagers and young adults staying here. Half of our staff are young people trying to either escape their lives or get back to their homes."

"I'll move her again," Simms reminded his friend. "Your family could get caught in the crossfire."

"*Neh.* My family comes and goes. Other than Agatha, they are all grown and they've been taught how to protect themselves. Living here, with the *Englisch* and their spring breaks, we've learned a thing or two. We are ever-aware."

Simms leaned back in his chair and crossed one booted foot over the other. "Sometimes that's not enough."

"I agree. Maybe we all took on too much, but we can't abandon Blythe. If you take her out of here, she won't be safe at all. So far, you've managed to keep them away."

"And how long can I keep doing that? It's too risky, Edward. I was wrong to bring her here."

Edward stood and stretched, leaving his rocking chair swaying. "Simms, if you take that girl all over Florida, she'll never recover. She'll be looking behind her always. You can't do any more than you're doing right here, right now. And out there, she is for certain sure more exposed. Here, she has half a dozen people watching over her."

"But she was in the line of fire today, and she had a panic attack. She's regressing instead of improving, and it's because her nightmare isn't over."

"And yet, you held your promise and you were here to protect her."

"Still, I can't give her the answer to her question. How do these people keep finding us?"

Edward thought about that. He sat back down and rocked, silent for so long, Simms thought he'd dozed off. Finally, he lifted up in his chair and turned to give Simms an ominous stare. "What if they got to someone who works here? What if they're paying someone off?"

Blythe had suspected that, but Simms hadn't brought it up with Edward. This operation ran like a well-greased engine. Edward didn't put up with slackers, or troublemakers.

"Blythe mentioned that," he told his friend,

"but I didn't follow through because the only missing piece is how did they know we were bringing Blythe here in the first place?"

"If these people are professionals, or military, as you've assumed, they'd have all kinds of ways to track someone."

"They'd need eyes everywhere," Simms replied. "I don't get it, and I'm more aggravated by the minute. The department worked hard to put away the people involved with Hayden Meissner's organized crimes. Now I'm guessing we didn't get all of his employees."

"Then we do what we can to bring them to us," Edward replied. "Lure one of them here and get the truth."

"That could be very risky," Simms said. "But I can start over and try to find out if anyone back in Campton Creek has military ties. Jeremiah Weaver might be of help. He left the Amish and joined the Navy, but he returned and is a faithful man now if ever there was one."

Edward frowned. "Perhaps he might not want to be involved?"

"*Neh*. He's a good man and he's helped a lot of people. He knows how these things work." Hope lifted Simms's worn, tired heart. "And I do know a couple there—not Amish, but they have Amish ties. He's a detective and she's a lawyer, married to each other now. If we all put our heads together, we might come up with something."

Edward nodded then gave Simms a shrewd glance. "Does this mean a trip home for you?"

"I don't know. I can't leave Blythe."

"*Ach, vell,* we could watch after her."

"I know you think I need to make amends with my father, but that is water under the bridge. He wants no part of me."

"How do you know that?" Edward asked, his tone quiet but full of understanding. "Have you talked to him?"

"I'm a prodigal, so no, I have not talked to him. It's no use."

"There is always time to mend fences," Edward said. "Think about it, but also do what you must to keep Blythe safe. That woman is just begging for a home and a lot of love."

Simms couldn't admit it, but he wanted to beg for the same thing, and being around Blythe again only reinforced that longing. He'd pledged to help her, but once this was over he had to let her go.

"I'll think on all of this," he told his friend. "Starting right now. I have a few calls to make."

"Maybe those calls will give you the information you need and you won't have to make this trip. *Gott*'s will can take time."

Simms left the main house and headed for the

grossdaddi haus. Dana was with Blythe, and they had an officer walking the perimeter of the two homes and the immediate grounds. The captain had also approved the team's request to use horses and four-wheelers to patrol the interior of the woods, since no vehicle could make it back into the swampy landscape just past the small lake.

His mind whirled with these new angles, and he knew sleep wouldn't come easily. He'd talked to Dana and Blythe but he wouldn't tell Blythe he might have to go back to Campton Creek until he knew for sure that would be necessary.

She might want to go, too, and there was no way he'd let her get near that town right now. Maybe Edward was right. Maybe she should stay here and remain near the main house.

Right now, taking her somewhere else could make things worse. But if he left and something happened to Blythe or any of the Klassens, Simms would never forgive himself.

Two days later, Blythe glanced up when Simms knocked on the back door of the cottage. He'd insisted on sleeping on the couch instead of inside the barn, and she and Dana had shared the bedroom. They'd had a quiet couple of nights, but Simms had left without a word each day before Blythe got up. He'd stayed busy with the animals and had helped clear some timber and shrubs around the house. When he did come to supper, he'd eaten and talked a little, then he'd gone off with his phone.

What was going through his head? What was he holding back?

Now, after a day when she'd stayed busy in the main house and had supper with the Klassens and only returned to the cottage a few minutes ago, Simms had managed to stay gone even though he was on the property. She had questions, but his gaze showed a weariness that was endearing, and yet disturbing. Blythe wanted to wipe that tiredness away, so she tried to be upbeat.

"Hello," she said, her nerves still shaky. "Would you like a cup of coffee or maybe lemonade?"

Simms studied Blythe with such intensity, Dana stood and yawned. "I'm going to put on my sleeping clothes. I don't like dresses, and this one is getting on my last nerve."

"Uh-huh," Simms replied, his gaze still on Blythe. "Thanks for filing your report so quickly. I'll go over things with you before we call it a night, so don't fall asleep yet."

"You got it," Dana replied. "Blythe, I'll be in the other room if you need me."

"*Denke*," Blythe said, her eyes never leaving Simms.

"I plan to sleep on the porch tonight," he announced.

Dana whirled around, her dress lifting out behind her. "Why not on the couch?"

"It's nice out," he replied. "I'll take a pillow and a quilt." Then he shrugged. "Bloomer will probably keep me company."

"Your choice," his friend said, leaving them alone.

Blythe knew these two talked in code. Maybe he'd open up if she didn't start asking questions.

Simms sank down across from Blythe. "Our officers checked the whole acreage again, going deeper into the thicket near the other side of the lake. They found footprints and off-road tire tracks in the pastures and woods. No fences there because it's marshland and hard to fence."

"That's the land out beyond the lake?" Blythe's heart did a quick sputter. "Swampy."

"Yes," he replied. "I hope to hear by tomorrow about the car that rammed us, and hopefully find prints, so we can start unraveling this situation."

"Like taking a messy stitch out of a quilt, ain't so?"

"This is one messy quilt, Blythe."

She sensed he needed to say more. "What are you not telling me, Simms?"

He gave her that blue-black stare she'd come to understand. "We think part of the Meissner organization is still out there. Based on some names that popped up in the database, some of his faithful cronies have come to the surface."

Blythe let go of a breath. "And they are gathering to attack me? I can see that for myself," she said. "I hear things and I know things. This is way past someone wanting to harass me again. This could become worse than what I've already been through."

"Not if I can help it." He stood and paced. "I think it all starts back in Campton Creek. I believe, as we suspected, your aunt could be involved."

TWELVE

Blythe gripped the arm of her chair. "I was afraid, but I kept telling myself she wouldn't do that. That she'd changed. I have not heard from her, but then, she is out of town and doesn't know where I am. I only left a brief message at the General Store telling him I had to go out of town." She stopped, her gaze hitting Simms. "Or does she already know I'm here?"

Simms held up his hand. "I haven't verified anything. I'm going with my gut here, so hold on. No one in New York has seen your aunt and her husband, and none of his family or any of the community up there can tell us their where-abouts. Either his family is covering for him or they're not in New York."

Frustration boiled over in Blythe's head. "What made you come to this conclusion if you don't have evidence?"

"Let's go over the timeline," he said, lifting a finger. "You noticed Arthur staring at you soon after he married your aunt. You began to feel as if something wasn't right. Rita wrote letters to Clara in prison and she visited Hayden in prison not long before he died."

"What? You left that part out."

"I just learned that today." He continued with the timeline. "Then Arthur and Rita decided to go visit relatives. A few days later you felt uneasy, and you thought someone could be watching you and might have been in your home. Then you found two men there and ran from them and, thankfully, got on a bus and made it down here. To me."

She let that "to me" comment slide over her like a soft wind.

"And I was followed and could have been killed but you showed up. That man got away and was later found dead, correct?"

"Yes." Simms studied her for a few seconds. "Yes. I believe they killed him because he didn't do his job."

"That was how Hayden handled things, so he must have planned this out. It's ironic that he died in the middle of his brilliant plans."

"Well, someone took over to finish those plans."

The air hissed while they stared at each other. "*Ja*, you are right. It's all adding up. Why else would *Aenti* go to see Hayden?"

"And why did he suddenly die the next day? I still believe someone slipped him an untraceable poison or managed to give him a true heart attack. If he thought you'd yet again betrayed him by storing up some of his fortune, he might have gone into a rage."

"I couldn't get to his money if I wanted to," she retorted. "Most of his assets were seized, as you well know." She stopped, put a hand to her lips. "But if someone indicated they planned to take his hidden money, he'd be helpless to stop them from prison. Or he'd die trying." Her eyes widened. "Simms, if he felt threatened he could have very well died a natural death. He always took pills for high blood pressure and he often told me he had heart problems."

"So that would establish how he died, but we have no proof of what your aunt or any other visitors might have told him." He jotted notes into his phone. "I'm going to have the prison go back over his visitors' list. We might have missed something."

"It makes sense," she finally said. "They must have tried to get to his money through him, but then he died. So they think I have money hidden somewhere, and the only way to get to it now is through me. Or over my dead body."

She put her hands together and stared down at the wooden floor of the tiny living room.

"Hayden had people working for him everywhere, Simms. Even the police—he paid them off to do his dirty deeds. If someone out there thinks I have hidden money, I won't ever be safe again."

"Someone sure knows how to find you," he replied, a dark rage forming on his face. "I think Meissner was putting tails on you from his jail cell. A narcissist like him would not forgive what you did. You made him look bad, and worse, your testimony sealed his jail cell door for a long time." He rubbed a hand down his shadow of a beard. "Your aunt could have stayed in touch with Meissner, to protect herself, but once he refused to cooperate, she and her new husband took matters into their own hands. Or maybe even before."

"You mean she'd give him information in return for his forgiveness after she bailed on him?"

"Yes. Forgiveness and hidden money to take care of you—alive or dead."

A clawing shudder of anger and fear moved down Blythe's spine. "Have you found out why she and Clara have written to each other?"

"Like with everything else, I'm waiting to hear. My guess is that your aunt needed information from Clara, so she started writing to her in hopes of getting just that."

"Then maybe we can get that information."

"That's the plan. The locals will send someone to talk to her, but she might not talk at all."

"Clara was so *gut* at covering her tracks, I doubt she'd offer up anything to help me. She hates me."

"But she hates prison more, I'm sure. We can offer to shave off a year or so."

"I'd rather she rots in prison."

He actually smiled. "You are one tough cookie."

Blythe took the compliment. "I should forgive her, I suppose."

Simms shrugged then rubbed his neck. "You can forgive, but you don't have to forget."

"I'll never forget."

"Blythe, I might have to go to Campton Creek."

"To find my *aenti*?"

"Yes, and to find her new husband. Surely they've returned from their so-called trip."

"If so, they don't seem worried about me, ain't so?"

"I have to agree. They probably thought they'd find you dead and they'd grieve without finding any explanations."

His gaze held her there, anger glowing in his frown and his stormy eyes. "No one would ever question them. They'd all sigh and say you had a lot of troubles and you associated with dangerous people."

Blythe saw the anguish beyond his anger. "You're thinking of your *daed*, aren't you? How no one could or would help him and he didn't fight for himself?"

Simms whirled around. "I'm thinking about how I want to wipe that fearfulness off your face."

Blythe sat still, weighing what to say next. A moment or two passed by as they gazed at each other. Her heart cried out while she dug her fingernails against her apron and tried to steady herself. This man made her weak at the knees.

She believed Simms couldn't and wouldn't say that he cared about her. This had become personal to him because of what he'd been through. He thought just as she did, that justice was hard to come by. But neither of them would give up on trying to find justice.

She looked away, knowing he would never confess that he cared. It was forbidden. He might have left the Amish but even now, he still respected their ways.

So she said, "I appreciate your protection, Simms. I have a feeling Arthur and Rita didn't plan to return. I have imagined every scenario, but I think we're onto the truth. They left, so someone could abduct me, get information, or whatever they needed, and Rita and Arthur would bide their time until they got word of my unfortunate death. They'd somehow get a fortune that I don't even know about, and they'd never return to Campton Creek."

"You should consider police work."

"I might need a job, that's for certain sure."

Simms finally sat down on the couch, close to where she held to the arm of her chair. He took her hand. "I don't want to leave you."

"Then take me with you."

"That would be too dangerous."

"And this isn't?"

His frown showed confusion. "That's a valid point but going back there could just bring more of them trying to get to you." He grunted, then leaned in. "We'll send a decoy with me if we decide to go that route. Dana or maybe someone who has dark hair like yours." His gaze slid over her *kapp* and then back to her eyes. "They'll think I'm taking you back, but if they try anything you won't be anywhere near me."

"What if this decoy gets shot or worse?"

"A trained officer will be aware."

Blythe thought about how she'd feel, being back where she'd been chased through the woods and almost taken. She had no real ties there anymore. Friends would worry, but most of the community had left her alone. Probably because of her reputation and her *aenti*'s constant nagging and complaining.

"I don't know that I want to go back there anyway," she admitted. "It's weird, but I do feel safe here. It's as if I've found the home I never had, you know?"

He smiled again. "This is a good family, no doubt about that. I'm glad you like it here."

"It's peaceful and productive," she replied. "Two things I'd like to be one day."

Simms's fingers were warm against her skin, his grip light like a whisper. He lifted his head and gave her a thorough perusal, his eyes losing some of their darkness. "So you're saying you'd be okay with me leaving, if it comes to that?" He let out a disgruntled breath. "I told you I'd stay here. I should consider how to handle this."

Blythe thought about all they'd been through. She cared for Simms and wanted to keep him near but being apart for a few days might help her to clear her head and get rid of this attraction she felt for a forbidden man. Could she stay safe, feel safe, without him near her?

Finally, she squeezed his hand, causing his eyes to widen like an eagle pondering the wide-open sky. "I'm a distraction. You don't need that when you're trying to gather information."

"You're not a distraction."

"I am, and you just won't admit it. When do you leave?"

His burning blue gaze stayed on her, allowing

her to see his mind percolating and processing, his frown softening, his eyes gleaming, his expression shadowed with flickers of hope as he calculated.

"I'd fly in—quicker that way—and use a rental car. I have some connections there—people who might be helpful."

"You could ask anyone about Rita and Arthur. They made a big show of going to church and helping out in the community. It was probably all fake, like my marriage was fake and my husband was a criminal who tormented and murdered people."

"Blythe?"

She stopped her rant, noticing he'd moved closer. "Simms?"

"Blythe—"

He gave her that look, the one where he didn't say what his expression was shouting. The look that caused her to melt and freeze all at the same time. Simms was the wrong person to make her feel like she might be floating, that new life flowed through her veins, and a new hope filled her heart, but here he was, his heated gaze burning through all the walls she'd built to protect herself. Confused, she struggled to find her next breath.

Blythe waited, knowing he would kiss her, hold her, comfort her. She stilled, her eyes closed while the scent of eucalyptus and lemons drifted from his clean skin to her turned-up nose.

Pounding footsteps caused Blythe to open her eyes and move away.

Dana came running out of the other room. "Fire! Simms, one of the produce warehouses is on fire!"

"Stay with her," Simms called to Dana. "Someone could be on the prowl just waiting to get inside the house."

He hurried out the door, tapping on his phone.

Dana went to one of the back windows and opened the curtain. "I saw it from the bedroom."

She wore sweatpants and a T-shirt now, her golden-brown hair long and curling over her shoulders. Blythe saw these details while her heart refused to accept the fire outside or the one inside her heart.

"They won't stop," she finally said as she moved behind Dana. The flames lifted out in the sky like a giant candle, flickering hot and hungry as the fire seemed to grow before their eyes. "They will not stop. What do they want from me?"

Dana came to her and hugged her. "You can do this, Blythe. You can fight back. We know your history, but you're a good person, and no one has the right to destroy or take your life."

Blythe embraced her new friend, thanking *Gott* for all her helpers and protectors. She pulled back to show Dana her gratitude. A whiz and hiss hit the air as the window glass shattered all around them.

Dana pushed Blythe to the floor, then fell down with her.

"What was that?" Blythe asked as they lay crouched under the window, shards of glass simmering over their clothes.

"A shot—with a silencer on the gun," Dana said, her hand going to the weapon at her waist. "Stay down, Blythe."

Blythe curled against the wall under the window. "You, too. Dana, don't go out there."

"That shot was for me," Dana said. "So they could get to you. Ain't gonna happen."

Blythe trusted Dana as a professional, but she worried about all of this. She didn't want blood on her hands. "Be careful," she said, deciding Dana wouldn't listen to her pleas. Her friend was trained to go after dangerous people. Blythe wished she wasn't here, crouched like a coward with glass broken all around her. She'd try to follow the protocol, so no one would get hurt.

Dana rolled and lifted, then offered her hand to Blythe. "Careful where you step. Did the glass get you?"

Blythe shook her head. "I don't think so. I'll clean up the floor."

"Forget that right now," they heard from the door.

Simms. Blythe held back a sob, seeing the courageous side of Simms as he moved with the instincts of a panther around the tiny house.

"Blythe, stay with me. Dana, I've called the fire department and alerted our guards. We've got backup coming from town."

"Roger that," Dana said, her voice calm, her eyes sparkling with an eager alertness. "Where do you want me?"

"With the family. Get them to safety until we find out who's out there."

Dana hurried out of the house, the familiar sound of fire truck sirens followed by cruisers jarring in the air. Blythe glanced out the window, the smell of smoke and charred wood drifting out in the moonlight. "This is terrible."

"It is. But again, they're trying to scare us and flush us out. I'm here with you. And I'm staying here with you."

She nodded, thinking that wouldn't help the Klassen family feel better. "What should we do?"

"Let's sneak you out to the main house. If Dana can keep the family contained inside the big house, I'll get an officer to take Edward to the warehouse. He wanted to take off down there on his own, but I told him to wait. My officer should be with him by now."

He went to the far window facing the warehouses and made a call, asking questions and giving out orders. "Check the perimeters and look for footsteps near all the entry ways. Make sure the gates are locked and ask the employees if they saw anyone hovering around."

"Edward is in good hands," he said to Blythe after ending the call. "Now let's get you into the main house where Dana and I can watch out for everyone."

He hurried to the back door and held her behind him as he scanned the space between the cottage and the house. "Stay off the porch until we're near the kitchen door. I'll let Dana know I'm bringing you over." He got close and looked into her eyes. "And remember, no matter what, you run to safety, okay?"

Blythe only nodded, her heart hurting while her head told her she needed to get away from everyone she cared about, before someone got hurt or worse, died. She'd never be able to forgive herself if that happened.

Simms tugged her through the garden, keeping her head low, his hand splayed across her *kapp.* More shots rang out, causing him to pull her close against the wall of the main house.

"They're not giving up," Simms said, his voice gravelly.

"They won't," she whispered.

Blythe stayed quiet and allowed Simms to lead her to safety. He motioned her up onto the porch between the two houses and tapped the door of the dark kitchen. Dana immediately opened it.

"All clear," she said, hurrying them in while she scanned the murky darkness behind them. "Edward is with Officer Hendrick. I've got people going after the shooter."

"Good," Simms told Dana, then he nodded to Cora. "Everyone here all right?"

Cora's worried frown said it all. "We're fine, just concerned for our warehouse and our safety. Our boys are with their *daed*, and Amy is with Agatha upstairs. We didn't want to scare her." She glanced around. "I'm worried about Bloomer. He usually alerts us if someone he doesn't know is on the property."

Dana pulled out her phone. "I'll ask around and see if anyone's seen Bloomer."

Blythe immediately went to Cora. "I'm so sorry."

"It's okay," Cora said, hugging her close. "Let's hope no one is hurt. We have insurance, but this will be a setback. We've always managed to get through such things."

Until now. No one had to say it, but he saw the regret and grief on Blythe's face. She thought their generosity might not last forever.

Before he could reassure her, two young men came running down the stairs.

"We should be out there helping Eddie and Terrance," one of them said.

Cora shook her head. "Adam, we've been over this. You two are to stay near the house. And you know why, don't you?"

"He's the one who took the fresh bread," the one she'd called Adam replied, his voice rising.

Cora stared at the other one. "Is that true, Jeffrey?"

"I was hungry," Jeffrey said. "That trip with Mr. Watson was hard work and he barely fed us."

"He was on a tight schedule," Cora replied. "But right now, I'm not worried about your bellies. You can't help with this situation, and I'm worried enough without having to ponder about you two getting into trouble."

Simms watched this encounter with interest, noting these two were full-grown teenagers. The two who Cora and Edward had mentioned were away on a delivery. They'd obviously just gotten home today. His radar went up immediately.

Cora motioned to them. "You can stay here

and help Detective Bueller watch out for any intruders."

"We might get shot," Jeffrey said, rolling his eyes. They both seemed to have an attitude that didn't fit in with this loving family.

Simms towered over them. "You will surely get shot if you run off into the night. Now, settle down and shelter here until this is over. If you want to help, act like men and watch over Cora and Blythe."

He studied them, taking in their tousled hair and old work clothes. They glanced at each other before noticing Blythe, something secretive passing between them, something that Simms could tell was causing her anxiety to go to the high mark. Adam gave her a sneer of a glare and nodded at her, his eyes holding disgust. "All of this is your fault, right?"

THIRTEEN

Blythe's breath left her body. How did these two know anything about her? "I beg your pardon?"

"When we got back late last night, we heard you were here," Adam replied. "I remember seeing you in the news. You turned on your husband."

Simms moved between them and Blythe, his frown growing darker by the minute.

"I…" Blythe couldn't move, the old dread pouring over her like hot molasses. "I…had no choice but to do the right thing."

The young man's dark eyes widened and so did the smirk on his face. "Then why are you still in trouble?"

"That will be enough, Adam," Cora said in a sharp voice Blythe had never heard before. "You mind your own business. Blythe, just as you are, is a guest in our home."

Jeffrey let out a grunt. "We don't want to be here, but we have nowhere else to go. Maybe that's why she wound up here, taking advantage."

"And you're not?" Mira asked from the kitchen. "You both know how *Mamm* and *Daed* feel about rudeness. This is our home. We invited Blythe here."

Adam rolled his eyes. "Well, her being here has invited trouble, for sure."

Adam was right, of course. "I guess trouble seems to find me," she said. "But we are blessed that these people want to help us, ain't so? I'm thankful for that, and you should be, too."

"Right," Jeffrey replied in a sarcastic tone. "*Ja*, this is for certain sure a paradise."

Simms stepped toward the boys, his frown slashing shadows across his face. "As Cora said, that will be enough. Either sit down and stay out of the way, or I'll take you both to my house and put you to work. Or maybe you'd like a ride to the police station."

Adam stared back at Simms, a daring glare in his eyes, but he didn't win. Simms stood stoic and stone-faced while Adam shifted and shuffled, his smirk turning to a pout. "Jeff, let's go back upstairs. It's quieter up there."

Jeff followed his buddy, the rest of them staring after them. But Blythe didn't miss the way Adam glanced back with a slight grin. Neither did Simms.

"I sure don't trust those two," he said on a low growl.

"I don't either," Mira replied. "That's why we keep them close and never let them anywhere on the property without a trusted employee chaperoning them. I should find out how things went on that delivery."

"I'll be watching them, too." Simms headed toward the windows, checking on the warehouse. "The fire has died down. Hopefully, they got it contained."

"You should be out there," Blythe said. "I'll be fine here."

"No." He paced like a trapped tiger. "The others know what to do, and the fire department crew will let us know if they find foul play. If I get too far from here, the intruders might try to harm all of you."

She didn't argue with him. His presence had always made her feel safe, but she reminded herself that her life wasn't her own. What plan did *Gott* have for her if she survived this? Or maybe she wasn't meant to survive this.

"Come and sit," Cora said, her own exhaustion showing in her gravelly voice. "It's been a long week. Let's pray in silence for those fighting the fire. And for my boys and Edward."

Blythe bowed her head and shut her eyes, her prayers a loud plea shouting inside her foggy brain. She tightened her eyes to avoid crying. Then she felt a warm hand moving over hers.

She opened her eyes. Simms. He had his eyes shut, too, but he'd managed to come and stand by the chair she'd sank against.

No one said anything. The few minutes of silence brought Blythe a bit of peace. This place held a certain tranquility that she'd never experienced before. She could easily stay here and never go back into the world out there.

But too much had happened. She needed to convince Simms to take her somewhere far away. Or she needed to slip away and hide somewhere, maybe even leave the Amish.

She lowered her head again but watched Simms. He must have felt her staring. He glanced at her with such an intense look that she almost bolted. That much longing and awareness in those sea-deep eyes scared her. She knew what marriage could bring but hers had not brought out feelings such as these. Remembering how revolting Hayden made her feel, she shuddered. She didn't have any bad feelings when Simms was near. More like, she wanted him to stay near her. The awareness of him being so close troubled her as much as not having him around, but it was the kind of trouble her heart wanted to happen. Her head told her to let him be, but her heart said stay strong and fight for true love.

But that would never happen once he caught the people tormenting her. Simms lived to catch criminals, and the adrenaline rush would be over once he'd done that. He'd see her on her way to wherever she planned to go. Nothing more.

Simms, for all his gruff and bravery, would be a gentle husband for someone. If he ever found that someone.

He lowered his head, a lock of dark hair shuttering his eyes. "Blythe, what do you want me to do?"

She had so many thoughts running through her head, so many dreams of sweet longing, she almost didn't answer. "There is nothing else to do but run away again, Simms. Far away. I won't put this family in danger anymore, no matter what they say."

He sighed and gave her a resigned nod.

Then the back door opened, and Bloomer came running inside and with a soft bark, headed right toward Cora. Terrance and Eddie pushed past Dana and the big dog. "*Mamm*, it's *Daed*. He's been hurt in the fire."

Cora ran toward the door, Mira following. "We must see about Edward," Cora called out, never stopping. "Make sure Amy and Agatha are okay, Simms."

"I'll go with them," Dana said. "You stay with Blythe and the children."

Simms nodded then started giving orders on his phone. "Be aware," he called after Dana as she guided the two upset women out the door. He turned to check on Blythe. She'd sat back down in her chair, her head down, her eyes closed. Bloomer ran to her and started nudging her hand. She gave the dog a soft pat on the head but never opened her eyes.

Simms said his own prayers but kept talking on the phone. "How bad is it?" he asked his contact at the burn site.

Blythe lifted her head, her dark eyes wide with questions. "I'm going to check on Amy," she whispered, not waiting for him to respond.

"Okay, keep me posted." He ended the call and turned back to Blythe just as she bustled down the stairs.

"Did you find everyone safe up there?" he asked as he rushed to the windows and checked the outside gas lights.

She blinked and looked around. "Amy and Agatha are asleep, but Adam and Jeff are gone." Then she pointed up the hallway to the other side of the house. "Simms, there's a smaller stairway near that big storage pantry in the back. It leads to another door out."

Simms ran to the pantry and then back toward

her. "The door is open, and I think Bloomer got out, too. I checked that door earlier, but they slipped away after I'd cleared it and that can't be good." He pivoted. "They might have let Bloomer go with them to keep him from barking while they escaped."

Blythe's eyes widened in fear. "You don't think…"

"I'm going to find out," he said. "I know their full names and I'm going to see what else I can find out about them. I didn't like the way Adam addressed you. He shouldn't even know why you're here, but somehow he did."

"People talk," she replied. "I'm surprised more haven't said something. Some think I'm a hero and some think I'm a lying traitor because I betrayed my husband."

"Your husband betrayed you and everyone else, so you don't need to think that way."

He paced and made another call. "I need background information on two Amish youths, Adam Hammond and Jeffrey Wilson." He described the young men with a honed precision and gave their last know location. "They might have records—petty theft and misdemeanors."

He reported the two teens were staying at the Klassen Farm and had been out of town recently delivering produce, and now they'd disappeared. After he hung up, he paced again. "I need to question the trucker who took them with him. This could be the source of all our woes."

Blythe glanced around, her hands together over her apron. "Those two could easily have been involved. They made it clear they don't approve of me." She shivered and shook her head. "They weren't here when Bloomer got into the cottage the other day, so maybe we're wrong."

"Well, until we have proof from the truck driver that they were with him for two days, we can assume what we want. It would have been easy for those two to sneak back in. The workers might not have noticed they'd even left. Only the family would have known that for sure."

"So you're thinking what I'm thinking," Blythe replied. "The dog and the bomb—possibly planted by them. What if the driver was in on it?"

"I'll check to make sure the shipment arrived," he said, jotting notes onto his phone. "And I'll get to the bottom of where those two are. I've got people on it already but so much is happening and I think this is just the beginning. It might be time to move you again, Blythe."

"I was going to suggest that anyway," she admitted. "I need to go where no one else can get hurt or killed, Simms."

"We might be grasping at straws," he said, "but we have to turn over every rock and con-

sider everyone who comes in contact with you."
Then he gazed at her, his frown deepening. "And
yes, we need to find a way to get you out of here
unseen. But remember this, wherever you go,
I'm going with you. That's not negotiable."

"Okay, we'll find somewhere to go—but this
time, Simms, let's get out of Florida. Let's find
a way to end all of this."

"I'm working on that," he said. "And I'll keep
working on it, even if I get kicked off this case."

"You might lose your job."

"We'll deal with that when it happens. I need
to make some more calls."

Blythe stood and went to the kitchen. She
grabbed the water pump to wash dishes and
started a kettle for hot water, just as she'd done
back home and in her own home. Except Hayden
demanded running water and regular bathrooms.
The best of everything and all of it bought with
ill-gained money. She filled the sink and then
turned when the kettle started whistling.

"You don't need to do that," Simms told her
in a quiet whisper after he'd put away his phone.

"*Ja*, I do need to do this. I need to stay busy
and grow tired and smile before I go to sleep, but
these nightmares, these happenings and this life
keep me awake with fear and dread and shame,
Simms. I need to wash the dishes."

He didn't say a word. Instead, he came over to

stand by her, taking the dishes to dry them and stack them while she scrubbed away her frustrations. When they'd run out of dishes a half hour later, he took the damp rag and dried her hands then tugged her toward the sofa in the big den.

"Now we rest."

Blythe wanted rest. How she wanted rest. She settled on the old worn couch and thought of this family, happy, healthy, hardworking, and how they gathered every evening for supper and helped each other through thick and thin.

She wanted that kind of life. She prayed for that kind of life. Then she turned and saw Simms watching her.

"I don't know if I can truly rest at all until people leave me alone and let me get on with my life."

"You can rest here, now," he said. "While I watch out for you."

He tugged her into the crook of his strong arm. Blythe shifted against him, letting his strength wash over her while she hoped she could give him a bit of softness. He'd given up a lot when he'd jumped the fence, and he'd rearranged his whole life for her. The man sure had a lot to prove, but he didn't have to prove anything to her.

But she still had questions. She scooted to the other side of the big sofa. "What about our plans? What about the missing teens and the truck driver?"

"I have to wait for the techs to get back to me with all the answers I've slammed them with. As for our plans, that's a fluid situation, subject to change at any moment. Just rest. I'll be right here, thinking it through." He pulled a quilt from the back of the sofa. "Get some rest."

He moved to the kitchen table and pulled out his phone.

Within seconds, she snuggled against a pillow and tugged the soft quilt up to her chin, her head turned toward him, her eyes closed, the image of a happy family moving through the dark corners in her mind.

To sleep, she thought. To sleep knowing she was loved and cherished and happy. If only that could be the way of things, if only Simms could be Amish again and she could walk without fear toward a life with him.

Was that just a silly dream? Would she live to find out?

Simms stood and checked on her. "Blythe?"

"Don't," she whispered, looking up at him. "Don't tell me this is wrong. Just for a few moments, Simms, let me stay here where I feel safe."

She heard his sigh, but she also saw the weight of his protection and his acceptance. They had something brewing between them, something real, something sweet and something dangerous.

It would end, of course. It had to.

But for now, with the world falling apart around them, she could have this one bit of quiet contentment before she faced the horror of her past and what might be in her future.

She could only hope that the Klassens' warehouse would survive and Edward would be all right. Her thoughts roiled and boiled, going back to the day her parents died and how she and Adina had been forced to live with their bitter *aenti*. How different their lives could have been if *Mamm* and *Daed* hadn't died.

But then she would never have met Simms or the Klassens. Maybe she had to go through all this torment to find her true self and to find her one true love.

Did she love Simms? She could be falling for certain sure. Soon, she'd have a different kind of torment—that of a heart broken over and over again, so she couldn't fall for Simms.

She'd have to put these mixed-up feelings out of her head, no matter how much she wanted it to be so.

An hour later, the doors crashed open and everyone starting talking at the same time. Blythe came out of her dream like a bird being set free.

"Edward has been taken to the hospital with a

broken leg and some minor burns," Dana called, ignoring the way they both sprang up from the couch. "We can't locate the two missing boys, but I put out the BOLO as you requested. Mira and Cora left in a patrol car, headed to the hospital to be with Edward."

Eddie and Terrance came inside smelling of smoke, their faces and clothes dingy with smut.

"The fire started near the freezer room, but it's contained," Eddie said. "We've lost some of a good amount of our produce, and we have a major shipment due tomorrow."

Terrance ran a hand over his face. "*Daed* always does this run because it's a big one, and my brother and I have only recently learned to drive the smaller vehicles," he explained. "It's a delivery to one of our biggest clients. I don't know how we're going to get the produce there in time."

"I do," Simms said. "I'll make the run."

Blythe turned to him. "And I'll go with you."

They'd just found the perfect front to get them on the road and away from this farm.

FOURTEEN

"You shouldn't be out there in the open, but this could be the best solution to us leaving," he replied, wondering how to help his friend and protect Blythe, too. "I could take you to Adina and Nathan's house."

"*Neh*, I told you I don't want them involved."

The same argument they'd had many times. Simms turned to Terrance. "Give me the details of this shipment."

"It's for a big hotel in St Petersburg. They like fresh produce, and they squeeze fresh orange juice every day, so we have a routine weekly delivery that either *Daed* or one on the older part-timers takes on. But since Curtis just made that long run with Jeff and Adam, he's not answering his phone. The boys told me earlier today he was sick. He left the delivery truck near the warehouse and went home, according to what they told me. Besides, we have to use the big refrigerator truck for this delivery. The produce has to be fresh, and enough to last at least a week. It's about thirty-five miles or more, and *Daed* can usually make the trip there and back in a few hours."

"Those boys are now missing, too," Simms told Terrance. "I need to question them, and I have people looking for them right now. But Edward needs my help, too. I think this could work if we can use this delivery to our advantage."

Terrance named the resort in St Petersburg. Simms knew the place well. A beautiful old paradise and a busy beach destination all year long. "So a one-day run?"

"At the most, in and out, and back," Terrance answered. "Even if we could make it, *Daed* wants us to stay here with *Mamm* when she gets back. And we can't leave Amy and Agatha, especially if Adam and Jeffrey are missing. That's trouble on top of trouble."

"Yes," Simms said, his nerves twitching with a bad feeling. "I think those two are up to no good, so I plan to question Curtis about their delivery trip. See if they mentioned anything about Blythe or Hayden Meissner."

Dana came in and heard most of the conversation. "We haven't found the source of the fire, but the fire department is going to go over the building again come daylight. The fire inspector will be back then."

Simms nodded, his bones weary, his mind spinning. "These people know how to cover their tracks, so we might not ever find an accelerant or anything else to show how they managed this." He glanced at Dana. "Did you question the night shift?"

"Yes, and no one saw them coming or going." Dana paced around the kitchen and den. "Plus, Adam and Jeff are still missing. I don't think that is a coincidence."

"I believe those two know more than they are letting on," Eddie said. "I've never trusted them, and now my instincts are telling me I'm correct on that."

Simms grunted, mad at himself for not vetting the young men more. "I need to check and see if our tech department has found anything on their backgrounds, and I'll send someone to check on this Curtis fellow, too. Let me make a call." He called in to the station, giving them Curtis Watson's name and last known location.

Then he pivoted and put his hands on his hips. "They're still searching for records on the missing teens, and they'll send a patrol to Watson's home for a welfare check. I was planning on how to move Blythe again, to get her out of this area. Your folks have done all they can, and it's too dangerous now. Terrance, get the shipment ready and I'll deliver it. Blythe will go with me, disguised as an *Englisch* woman."

He turned to Blythe, his mind at war with his soul. He couldn't leave her here. Yet he was afraid to take her away from this farm. "After the delivery, Blythe and I will leave the truck where you can find it. But you won't be able to find us."

"This is a *gut* plan, Simms," Blythe said, her expression waffling between anticipation and apprehension.

"Well, right now it's the only plan we've got."

He pondered all the reasons she should hide here, but then thought of all the reasons he didn't want her out of his sight.

With another grunt followed by the breath he'd been holding, he looked over at her. "You can ride with me only because I won't leave you here alone, especially with Adam and Jeff missing. Dana and the other officers will watch out for the family, just as we've discussed."

Blythe didn't speak but she acknowledged him with a slight nod. He was letting her know he meant business. Doing his job to the bitter end. "Maybe if I'm not here, they'll be okay and this place will go back to being peaceful and happy."

He rubbed the back of his neck. "I've about stretched the department to its limit on getting more officers out here, but we'll continue with the guards at the front gate and around the perimeters until Edward can come home." Touching Terrance on the arm, he asked, "You both know how to use a shotgun, right?"

"We use rifles and shotguns for hunting, *ja*," Eddie replied. "You aren't suggesting we shoot anyone, are you?"

"No," Simms said, lifting his hand. "I'm only suggesting you be prepared and use those weapons wisely."

"You mean, to save someone they might harm?" Terrance asked, his dark eyes full of worry and determination.

"Exactly," Simms said. "Self-defense if needed."

Dana lifted her chin, her words bringing Simms back to the present. "I'll do most of the shooting, but it's good to have backup."

Simms gave them all a sweeping glance, but he wanted them to understand. "This family has gone beyond their duty for us, so we can't let them down. And I won't tolerate these attacks again. I hope to hide Blythe somewhere else, but if they do happen to see Blythe and me leaving, maybe we can draw them away from here and capture them. Especially if we have an unmarked car tailing us when we make this delivery."

"That's a long shot," Dana said, but her eyes held pride. "We'll be careful, Simms. They haven't won yet."

"Let's hope they never do," he replied. Then he turned to Blythe. "Are you sure about this?"

"*Ja*, I want to get away, but if they follow us and try another attack, I want them to get caught and pay for their crimes." She glanced out at the night. "I need my life back and I need for the Klassens to feel safe again."

"Okay. We'll leave before daylight," Simms said. "Right now, I'm going to look around the property for Adam and Jeffrey. They left in a hurry for a reason, but we have a BOLO out on them. Dana took care of that."

"What's a BOLO?" Eddie asked.

"Be on the lookout," Simms explained. "Every law enforcement agency in the state will be watching for them."

"And we'll have our own BOLO here," Terrance added. "I hope we find Bloomer soon, too. I'm worried he's following Adam and Jeff around. They like to give him treats."

"Exactly, and all the more reason to find all three of them." Dana stopped her pacing. "I'll keep Blythe here in the main house for now. No telling how long you'll be before you actually get in the truck and go. Safety in numbers and all that."

"I agree. Stay alert and only let in people you know are cleared. Get some rest."

Terrance turned to Simms. "I'll come with

you and help look for Adam and Jeffrey, then we can load the truck. You can head out before sunrise and get back home before dark."

"It's a risk," Simms admitted, turning to Blythe again. "You can wear a baseball cap to hide your dark hair. Hopefully, we'll make the trip without any surprises and that will be that, and if not, we'll at least lure them away from here, have people tail them and finally catch them. If I leave Blythe here, however, she's still exposed and so are all of you, as we've seen."

"Take her," Dana said, her chin up. "She feels safer with you, Simms, and I'm here to handle the rest. Unless you want me to take the truck."

"*Neh*," Terrance said. "*Daed* is particular about this and Simms has helped us out before."

"I'm paying back a friend," Simms said. "And I'm protecting a friend while I do it."

"Then it's settled," Blythe said, sighing. "It will be good to have a break and give this family a break."

Dana checked the washroom. "Great. Cora washed the jeans and shirt I wore yesterday and they're clean and dry. We're about the same size but these might be baggy on you, so put them on. I'll find you a hat somewhere."

Eddie pointed to the mudroom. "All kinds of hats in there. People tend to leave them behind."

Simms only hoped he wouldn't regret this

risky decision, but what choice did he have? He didn't trust anyone else to protect Blythe, and yet the hits kept coming so he obviously wasn't much of a protector himself. But they had thwarted the enemy several times. He had to believe he was doing the best he could.

And he had to believe he could keep Blythe alive, no matter what came at them next.

Eddie woke Blythe at dawn.

When she entered the kitchen a few minutes later, he handed her a to-go cup of coffee and two ham-and-cheese biscuits.

"For the road," he said, whispering, his gaze dancing over her outfit—old jeans and a T-shirt embossed with palm trees and blue water. "Simms is up and drinking his *kaffe* already. I'll stay here with Dana, Amy and Agatha. They'll have questions. Terrance will be in charge of the other employees, and they'll start cleaning up the burned part of the warehouse once the fire marshal and our insurance agent both look it over. I haven't heard from *Mamm*, but I imagine she'll send Mira home later."

Blythe nodded, her body tense with anticipation and agony. She'd prayed all night, asking for safety. She hoped the people after her would be caught today. At least a road trip with Simms would get her away. And it might do both of them good after all the happenings around here. She figured Simms would rather be in the thick of things regarding the fire and all the other things that had happened, but until he got enough evidence to pin down her pursuers, he could only help out around here.

Delivering this load of produce would be his way of doing something significant to repay his friends. Her going along for the ride was his way of watching out for her and accepting that she needed to be somewhere else. The added bonus would be if they did lure these criminals out of the shadows. Being in a big truck could protect them and give them a chance to stop these attacks. If this didn't bring out her tormentors, Blythe would have to find another place to hide. Maybe one where no one could find her. Not even Simms.

When she heard the roar of a truck motor, she gave Eddie one last glance. "We'll see you later today."

Dana came out of the downstairs bedroom and smiled then headed for the percolator full of coffee. "Your ride is here," she said, checking the yard that glistened a creamy yellow from the security lights. "Y'all be careful, and I'll hold down the fort here and watch out for Agatha and Amy. Terrance and Eddie will help, right, Eddie?"

"Right," Eddie said with a tight smile. "See you later, Blythe. Tell Simms *denke* from me."

"I will." She took the coffee and biscuits, waited for Dana to open the door and scan the area, hoping that Bloomer would return and that the boys would be found. Whether they were in on this or not, they needed to explain. She saw Simms coming around the huge purring truck to help her into the passenger-side seat, and her mind went straight to getting away with him.

Maybe this wasn't a great idea after all.

He lifted her like a sack of potatoes, nodded, and without a word shut the door, scanned the yard, then hopped back inside the massive vehicle. Blythe looked around, the big seat swallowing her. She glanced at Simms and saw his stony face in the shadows. He had a lot on his shoulders this morning.

"Buckle up," he said, his voice gravelly. "This is a sixteen-foot truck that can hold about four-thousand pounds, and we have it loaded to the gills with oranges and all sorts of fruits and vegetables. How you holding up?"

"And *gut* day to you, too," she said, remembering waking in the hospital to find him full of unleashed energy and their next plan. "I saw how big this thing is and soon realized I couldn't get into it by myself. I've never been in a vehicle like this."

He shifted the growling gears and guided the truck toward the gravel drive. "I've never had an assignment like this."

"You're being pulled in two different directions," she replied. "I don't know how I'll ever thank you, Simms."

He didn't reply right away. They were approaching the closed gates to the farm, two guards dressed in dark clothing waiting to let them pass.

After he'd talked to the two officers who knew him, he pulled the roaring monster out onto the highway and checked all the mirrors.

"You don't have to thank me," he finally said. "It's my job."

The man would never admit to anything other than his dangerous work. Did he have a death wish because he'd abandoned his people? Or had he abandoned his family because he had a thirst for adventure and danger?

"Do you go to all this trouble for anyone who needs help?" she asked, hoping to get him to open up since they were alone in a delivery truck.

"I try," he replied, glancing over at the towel in her lap. "Do I smell a ham biscuit?"

"Oh, I'm sorry. You're probably hungry."

"I am. You should eat, too."

"I don't know if I can. My nerves are like jelly."

"Try, Blythe. Cora's biscuits are the best around."

Blythe opened the towel and then lifted the foil off one of the flaky biscuits, thinking of sweet little Aggie and her pretend biscuits. She didn't get to say goodbye to her new friend. "Here's yours."

Simms took the big biscuit full of sliced ham. "*Denke*."

Blythe smiled at the thank you, then opened her coffee and took a long sip. "That's *gut*." She lifted the other piece of foil and grabbed the hefty biscuit. Taking a bite, she savored the ham and cheddar with a hint of spicy mustard on it. "That's *gut*, too."

Simms actually smiled. "We can pretend we're on a road trip to deliver fruit and life is great. We have food and coffee and the world is outside the confines of this heavy-duty truck."

"I'd like that," she said. "I didn't realize you know how to pretend."

"Blythe," he said, his voice low and full of tremors she couldn't figure out, "I've been pretending for most of my life."

Then he finished his biscuit and drained his coffee while the sunrise to the east moved up the sky like a giant beach ball, all yellow and pink and serene.

Blythe held this moment in her heart. A moment where she was with a man she cared about and respected, a moment where she could savor a biscuit and be with Simms. A moment where he'd revealed a lot in one ornery retort to her question. Simms put on a big show, but deep inside, he missed the old ways, the plain ways. This wouldn't last, of course. The people out there who wanted something from her, who wanted to destroy her, would find them again, and there would be no more pretending.

Just a stark reality that held her in its clutches like a hawk holding a dove. Would she ever be free? Would Simms ever be settled and happy or would he always mourn the life he'd left?

FIFTEEN

Simms didn't like all the feelings Blythe brought out in him. He'd never before told anyone he considered himself a pretender. Just saying that out loud made him mad. But if he were honest, and when was the last time he'd been that, he did feel like a fake. He'd left his life behind when he was nineteen and too puffed up with his own pride to realize his father had done the best he could do. He'd left his sister behind and his *mamm* had passed away two years after he'd left. Maybe that's why he couldn't go back. He'd loved his *mamm*, but she'd stood by his *daed* and Simms couldn't understand that.

Until now.

Because he'd chosen to stand by a woman who was a mystery to him and notorious within the Amish community. A woman who'd turned away from the luxury of being married to a wealthy Amish man because she'd discovered he was a dangerous, deranged criminal.

She could have stayed with Hayden and kept his dirty secrets, but she'd done the right thing.

"Did he abuse you?" Simms blurted out, thinking now he was saying out loud what he needed to keep to himself. Only, he also needed to know.

Blythe looked shocked—that he'd spoken and that his words concerned her husband—Simms figured. She also looked cute in a tan baseball cap with *Pass-a-Grille Beach* etched in pink and surrounded by grapefruit across the brim.

"Hayden?" she managed to say in a throaty question.

"Yes."

She shrank into the big seat, her gaze on the road ahead.

"Blythe?"

She finally turned toward him. "You know what he did."

"Not all of it. You don't talk about your actual marriage to the man."

"I'm trying to forget that part. All of it, really."

"I know it's personal and I shouldn't pry, but I need to understand how a man could do that to a woman—be mean and cruel and hurt her. How he could hurt you."

She slumped even more, making him feel awful for asking. So he focused on the vehicles behind them and, finding no tails or dark sedans, he relaxed and kept his mind on scanning the road, the cars, checking the mirrors, and wondering if they'd truly get a break. He had unmarked cars ahead and behind them, prepared for anything that might come.

"He hit me sometimes."

The whisper came like a shiver moving up Simms's backbone.

He couldn't speak through the anger that boiled over like lava through his veins.

"And he locked me in the bedroom a lot, to keep me subdued. He preached to me, told me I needed to be submissive, quoted the Bible and the *Ordnung* to me, and sometimes, he'd have me repeat back what he'd said so I could come out and have some food."

"What else?" Simms asked, gritting his teeth.

She glanced over at him, seeing the intensity of his feelings because he couldn't pretend with this. He couldn't hide the rage or the horror of hearing these things.

"I'd rather not say."

She didn't have to say. Simms swallowed the bile rising in his throat. "I'm glad you got away, Blythe."

"*Ja*, me too."

He reached his hand toward hers and waited. Finally, she took it, her fingers intertwined with his, their softness warming his roughness, their warmth melting his frozen heart.

For a while, they held hands, silent. Then he glanced back and saw a black SUV barreling toward them.

"We're almost to the resort," he said, tugging his hand away, "and it looks like someone has spotted us."

Blythe sat up, blinked and said, "That didn't take long. But this time, I hope they're the ones who'll be surprised."

Simms nodded and hit the pedal. "Glad we have unmarked cars ahead of us and behind us."

"We do?"

He glanced over at Blythe. "It's the only way my captain would let me do this. But sometimes you have to do something risky to make everything right."

Like him thinking they had so much that should keep them apart, and yet he wanted to get to know her more and more as he spent time with her.

Simms eased off the gas and let out a deep breath as the SUV passed by and kept going. "False alarm. I tend to forget a lot of people drive black SUVs around here."

"Hayden had one," Blythe said, her heart settling back down to normal. "Dark windows, hefty men who chauffeured him around as if he were a king."

"Maybe he thought he was a king. But he's probably answering to that right now."

Blythe closed her eyes. "I wish I could get him out of my head."

She thought of what Simms had said earlier, about them just doing a job, delivering some produce, smiling, drinking coffee and eating a big biscuit. A normal, ordinary life.

"I wish I could stay with the Klassens forever," she said, not even realizing she'd whispered that out loud.

Then she opened her eyes and saw the huge white condo building rising above them. "This is different."

Simms gave her a guarded glance. "It's full of tourists, and everyone here has to have a pass to be inside these gates, but as I've said before, criminals can get around that."

Maybe he'd missed her vocal plea for a simple life. She hoped so. "We made it here safely," she said. "So what do we do now?"

He pulled the truck up to the gate and explained why they were here. The guard took his name and after calling someone, nodded them in. "You know where to go?"

"Yes, sir," Simms answered. Then he guided the rumbling truck to the right around a walled curve that led to the back of the sky-high building. "We'll unload in the back near the kitchen. We'll have help so we should be done within an hour."

Blythe glanced around, seeing the dark parking garages full of all kinds of vehicles, a chill moving through her at the thought of getting lost in one of those things. The huge high-rise made her dizzy, and her jingling nerves only added to that feeling.

"I'll be glad when we're back home. Wherever home might be."

Simms did glance at her then. "I know you love the Klassen place, but you'll be free to do what you want and you won't have to hide anymore once this is over."

"I'll always hide," she admitted. "I want the world to leave me alone for a long, long time."

He didn't say it, but she saw a wave of regret in his eyes. "I understand."

But did he? Could he understand the loneliness, the longing, to just be loved? To have a normal family? To be a good wife and mother, to be a member of a community where everyone cared about each other?

Glancing at him, she guessed he longed for such things but he held a wall of make-believe around those longings. Maybe he *was* just pretending. And maybe she'd been pretending to

be someone she wasn't when she married a sociopath.

She'd married Hayden for all the wrong reasons, and the same thing could happen if she
pined away for Simms. He wouldn't cave, but
she for certain sure could. The only thing worse
than marrying a criminal would be to abandon
the plain ways and stay with Simms.

She couldn't do that.

She didn't ask for an explanation about his
feelings. Instead, she watched as he maneuvered
the truck with ease, backing it up to a cement
warehouse dock where heavy plastic curtains
hovered and swayed across the open space they'd
move through to unload their haul.

Two workers came through the curtains to
greet them. Simms hopped out and ran around
the front of the truck to help her down, his hands
firm on her waistline as he lifted her and then
planted her onto the concrete, his gaze telling
her things he'd never voice.

"You okay?" he asked in a tight tone, his
hands still holding her near. "Just help as much
as you'd like but we'll do most of the heavy lifting."

Like he'd been doing all his adult life?

Blythe didn't want him to let go, but they had
work to do. "I'm fine. Let's get this done."

He pivoted and studied the two workers long enough for both men to get to work.

"Yeah, we'll get in, get out and be on the way to a location where I can leave the truck. We might make it through with no problems. Or we might be able to end this today, one way or another."

His phone buzzed and after checking the caller, he turned to Blythe. "I have to take this. It's from the private investigator I got in touch with back home in Campton Creek. That means he has some news for us."

"And that could be *gut* or bad," she replied as she watched their helpers opening up the truck.

Another shiver moved through Blythe as a dark cloud covered the sun and left the desolate loading platform shadowed in gray and blue. Just like everything she'd seen in life before she'd met the Klassens, this glamorous place held a façade that only a few could see through.

Simms ended the call with a dark scowl on his always mysterious face. His phone buzzed again, so he couldn't tell her what he'd found out. She kept watching and saw his frown go into a dark grim twist that she couldn't read.

After ending the call, he pushed at his hair and started unloading boxes of produce. When he didn't say anything, Blythe lifted a tray of lettuce and passed it to the two scrawny men working the loading dock. She'd keep quiet until they could have some privacy, but whatever he'd heard had obviously riled him up.

The fall sunshine was warm, but the Gulf breeze held a hint of winter, such as winter was on the peninsula of Florida. Blythe enjoyed the fresh air and the work, but her mind whirled with wondering what Simms had heard. It took them over an hour to get the truck unloaded, but that time seemed to stretch so long, Blythe thought she'd scream. Simms acted like a man who needed to be elsewhere. He lifted the produce boxes and almost ran through the flapping plastic blinds to get his haul inside. Something was up, but he wouldn't tell her here and now, when they were pretending to be delivery people.

Whatever it was, it couldn't be good news.

"We're done," one of the workers finally announced after Blythe's thoughts had gone numb. He shook Simms's hand. "Give my regards to the Klassens."

Simms gave the young man a cold stare, but he shook his hand. "I'll do that."

They signed off on the paperwork and the employee went back inside to the big refrigerator where they'd stored most of the produce. Simms moved to the far corner of the loading dock and made another call. Would she ever get to talk to him?

He finally walked over to her, his expression blank and stony.

"Hard to believe they'll need more in a week," she said by way of a conversation. "I suppose we'll be long gone by then."

Simms helped her into the truck without a word.

"Simms, what did you hear?" she finally blurted out. "I think I have a right to know."

Simms checked in with the officers in the unmarked cars parked near the loading dock, then cranked the big truck, revving the motor as he slowly moved it away from the back section of the high-rise condo.

"You do have a right to know, Blythe, so I'm just gonna say it. First, Curtis Watson was found dead in his home this morning."

Shocked to hear that, she gasped. "The truck driver?"

"Yes. Shot dead. Which means Adam and Jeff were lying to us when they told us he was sick."

"What else?" she asked, afraid to hear anything more.

Simms glanced down at his boots and then looked up to her. "I'm sorry to tell you this but your deceased husband has an illegitimate son, and the folks helping me think he's the one in charge of all these attacks on you. He's been trying to get to his father's money for years, and you're the last person between him and what he considers a fortune."

Blythe's breath left her body with a swish that sounded over the engine. Simms watched as she turned pale and looked as if she couldn't breathe. She didn't speak. One hand went to her mouth while the other landed on her heart, the terror in her eyes telling him everything.

"Blythe?"

She waved his concerns away, but she didn't speak.

He'd held off telling her because eyes and ears could be everywhere, even in this truck, which he'd discreetly checked before they'd finished unloading. He hadn't liked the message one of those men wanted him to send. *Give my regards to the Klassens.* How did that guy know the Klassens? Was it because he helped unload their products so he knew Edward, or had that been sent as a threat? It would have been easy for those two rowdy teens who had mysteriously gone missing to be persuaded with cold, hard cash to plant a bug in all the trucks coming and going through the farm. And that might explain how their enemy was always a step ahead of them. Including the time Bloomer wound up in the cottage and regarding the loading crew at the dock. Someone could have followed Simms to the Klassen's farm and seen Blythe with him. But how could they get to the boys unless they'd cornered them at a loading dock somewhere. That would explain why Curtis was murdered— he'd seen something.

Now, Simms had to focus on the next step to keep everyone safe. When he looked over at Blythe, her skin glistened with perspiration and her pupils were dilated. "Blythe, do I need to stop this truck?"

She finally glanced over at him, her eyes wide with fear, her breath shallow. "I can't—"

She was having a full-blown panic attack. Simms watched the traffic and pulled the truck over across from the resort gates into a souvenir shop parking lot. Careful to make sure no one was around or turning in after them, he killed the motor, and saw their detail cars circle back toward the parking lot. Turning to her, he put his hands on her shoulders, careful to be gentle so he wouldn't scare her.

"Blythe, breathe. You're with me. You're safe. Think of the farm and how you love it. Think of the smell of orange blossoms and honey, the bright colors of hibiscus flowers, of sunshine and people laughing. Breathe, Blythe. Breathe and look at me."

She finally looked into his eyes. Simms wanted to pull her close, but he knew that would only upset her more. Her gaze held a level of trust that made him feel humble and different inside, not so hard and locked inside himself.

"Just breathe," he whispered, keeping his voice low and soft. "Just keep breathing and keep your eyes on me."

A breath flowed, and another, and another. Her rigid body slowly went limp as she managed to relax.

Simms held the gaze, watching her for any reactions. Then he handed her a bottle of water. "Blythe?"

"I'm…okay," she finally said, her voice husky and low, but she had a little color back on her face. "Just shocked. A son? My husband has a grown son?"

Simms's heart crashed like a rogue wave growling at the shore. "He does, yes. He was definitely born before you met Hayden, from what my associates found out. And…he's *Englisch*."

"He's not Amish?" Tears flowed down her face now, but she recovered her shaky breath and took hold of the air flowing in and out of her body. "Hayden had an affair with an *Englisch* woman?"

"Apparently when he was very young, and it happened during his own *Rumspringa*. Maybe twenty from what we can tell. He sent money but he refused to marry the mother. The son wasn't supposed to ever find out about him, but somehow he did. Now, he's demanding the fortune he believes he should have."

So that meant Hayden's son was in his twenties, a little younger than Blythe. And he never once mentioned it.

"Hayden told me he couldn't have children. Now I know he just didn't want any children."

"Well, this young man is on a mission to get what he thinks should be his."

"And I'm standing in the way, he thinks."

"Yes. His name is Danny Lewis. He's an adult now and he has a nice bank account thanks to Hayden being so successful. So Hayden did provide for him. Personally, based on the numbers a friend found in the Lewis bank account, I think the mother might have started extorting Hayden after he made his fortune. The mother died a year before Hayden got arrested, so maybe Danny decided he'd keep up with the extortion, by taking you for ransom, or finding the funds and then disposing of you. His account has a fair amount, but the young man wants all of it, every last penny."

Blythe looked out the window and then back at Simms. "He has enough money to hire people to torment me and abduct me? Maybe even kill me and the people I care about?"

"He seems bent on getting to you, yes. I'm not sure how he's funding this. He could be paying some money upfront and promising the rest on the back side when he hits pay dirt."

"How can he do this? He doesn't know me. He has to know how evil Hayden was."

"He can only see that he never had a father growing up, and in his mind, he thinks he's owed the rest of the inheritance. I don't think he harmed Hayden, but I'm guessing he tried to get to the money after Hayden went to jail, and now Hayden has conveniently died so Danny is getting desperate."

"What if he did do something to Hayden?"

"It was a massive heart attack, and we have no evidence to show foul play." Simms paused. "Unless, like you suggested, someone—maybe his son—showed up and they had words and Hayden got so enraged, he had the attack. I'll check back with the prison to see if Danny Lewis ever tried to visit him." He held her hand, seeing the color was back in her face. "For now, however, we have a solid lead on who is behind this. Which means you're still his target."

"I don't have any of that money, Simms."

"We know that, but he is probably counting

on abducting you and forcing you to sign something over to him."

"And that's why I'm still alive?"

"I think so."

She glanced around as if she'd just realized they were sitting in a delivery truck at a tourist shop. Then she looked over toward the condos looming all around them. "Money truly is the root of all evil," she said. "I'll have none of it. Just get me out of here, Simms. I'll find a new life somewhere else."

"It won't be that simple," Simms said. "I think the man who married your aunt is working with him. It could be a scheme they came up with after they saw all this play out on the evening news. The shakedown, the trial, your image flashing across the screen, you turning on your husband. A lot to unpack there and a good motive for an illegitimate kid to take action, especially one who got used to Daddy's money coming in each month. Add that to the public's interest in Amish people, and he probably came up with a plan during the trial. But his *daed* died, and that left him floundering again. He didn't waste any time finding you."

"And probably the reason my *aenti* kept in touch with Hayden and Clara. Clara would know where the money is, but they can't get to her in prison."

"You're right there. I'm guessing they had Rita send her letters to see if she mentioned things regarding Hayden's hidden bank account, if there is one. So this is anything but simple, and I'm afraid we've only hit the tip of the iceberg."

"Simple," she said. "I only want a simple life and mine has been nothing but difficult since the day my parents were killed in that buggy crash."

"I wish it could have been different," he said, meaning it. He reached over and tugged at the silky strands of dark hair that had settled all around her baseball cap. "I wish I could change all that."

"*Gott*'s will," she said, closing her eyes. "That is what will change my life, Simms."

Simms couldn't argue with that. He said a prayer, asking God to show them His will. And soon. "We have to go."

She pushed at her hat. "*Ja.* I'm ready. But... did you hear anything about my *aenti*? Is she still caught up in this?"

He hated to tell her more bad news. "Your *aenti* and her husband are missing. No one knows what has happened to them. Even more concerning, we can't find any information on Arthur Glick. I think he's using an alias—a new name."

She looked up and directly into his eyes. "If she did this to me, if she is trying to find money

I don't have, I will never forgive her. Never. She married this man so quickly and probably because he promised to give her a better life. She doesn't really care about Adina and me, and now that's very clear."

"I agree," he said, because he couldn't understand how anyone could be that cruel. "But you should consider the other factor."

Blythe lifted her gaze back to him. "That they were collateral damage? That Rita and Arthur might be dead?"

"You understand collateral damage?"

"*Neh*, but I understand murder," she replied, her panic gone and a new determination gleaming in her eyes. "I understand a lot of things these days, Simms."

He needed to get this truck on the road and get her away from here. Time was running out on them. If Danny Lewis had somehow gotten to Adam and Jeff, and persuaded them to help him, those boys could still hurt the Klassens, or they'd be killed for not doing the job. But how could he get back to them and try to protect Blythe at the same time?

"I have to call Dana," he finally said. "The Klassens are still in danger."

He pulled out his phone and told Dana what he'd learned and explained the situation. "Keep searching for Adam and Jeffrey. I'll be back as soon as I can get there."

After he ended the call, Blythe stared over at him, her dark eyes like glistening onyx, her face set in a firm, tight resolve. "I've been so selfish. I only wanted to run away because I thought if I took myself out of the picture, the Klassens wouldn't be targets anymore. But they will always be targets because they've been involved with me. We have to go back, Simms. We have no other choice. I won't let anyone in that family die on my behalf."

SIXTEEN

Simms let out a grunt of frustration. "I agree we need to help Dana and the others, and now we have every reason to be concerned. Dana is aware and on it, but you're my priority right now. Let's get somewhere safe and I'll call in an alert to Captain Walker. He won't like me going rogue, but I'll deal with the fallout later."

"I don't care about my protection anymore," she replied. "We started this. We need to finish it. I wanted to run away but I can't leave that family helpless, and I know you don't want to either."

Simms tapped his fingers against the steering wheel with an impatient cadence, wishing she didn't have to be so noble. "Look, I admire your logic, but I still need to keep you safe. And the only way to do that is for us to keep moving."

"You have kept me safe, so many times," she reminded him. "But we can't keep running. We might not have flushed out these people chasing us, but what you just told me shows we're getting closer and closer to the truth. If those two teens are involved, they could be in jeopardy, too. We need them to confess and tell us the truth. I'm so worried. I can't stop thinking that while we're trying to get away, they'll come after innocent people to bring us back."

"And it's working because we are having this very discussion. They'll lure you back and then what?"

"I'll stand up to them. I don't know. I'll prove to them I don't have any hidden money."

"Then they will surely kill you."

She stayed still and quiet for only a moment. "Are you going to take me back, or do I have to hire a cab?"

He studied her, the tension in his body close to the breaking point.

Hitting the steering wheel with the heel of his palm, he said, "Okay, we'll get the truck back and I'll give a complete update to the station so we can get the evidence lined up. My friends in Campton Creek are searching for Danny Lewis and the Glicks, and they're gathering everything they can to help us."

"Okay, then let's go," she said, her gaze scanning the streets. "Now, Simms. I have a bad feeling about us leaving Klassen Farms."

Simms hit the gears and turned the truck back

onto the road. Then he radioed their escorts and told them they were heading back to the farm.

He scanned the road. "Our escorts are in place."

Blythe let out a breath and pushed at her hair. "*Denke.*"

They made it to a traffic light on a busy intersection when he let out groan and hit his hand against the steering wheel again. Then in the next second, he pushed Blythe's head down, causing her to briefly let out a gasp in protest.

"Stay down. We've been made."

Gunshots rang out. Blythe glanced at him. "Stay down, Blythe. One of the unmarked cars just got a tire blown."

"From a gunshot?"

"Yes, and we're next."

Blythe let out an angry cry, her rushed words boiling with rage. "I'm tired of this."

"You and me both," Simms responded. "Hang on and don't raise your head."

Blythe did as he said, but she twisted around to see Simms. He had his weapon ready but driving with one hand while he watched the SUV behind them wasn't easy. Bullets hit the metal bed of the insulated truck. Simms keep going but managed to shift the gun to his left hand.

"Simms?"

"It's okay. Our other protection detail has turned around. They know to cover us while

I get us out of here. I need to get this truck behind a building, and we're going to abandon it and run. You hear me, we run back toward the condos."

"If you say so." She took deep breaths and held his gaze. This truck was strong, but one bullet could end it all. "Blythe, do you understand?"

Her dark eyes burned with heat. "I'll run. But I'm still going back to the farm if I can find a way."

Simms fired at the approaching vehicle before turning into an alley lined with colorful beach cottages and quaint little homes. Then he slammed on the brakes. "Jump, Blythe."

She took a deep breath and opened the heavy door.

"Stay near the truck until I come around."

"Okay."

She dropped and crouched near one of the massive wheels, the sound of gunshots and bullets making her hold her hands to her head.

Simms reached for her while he shielded her. "I've got you."

"Let's go," he said. "We'll get lost in the condo crowds. Stay with me. If we get separated, it will all be over—and in a bad way."

He worried she'd think about going off on her own now. Too dangerous and in a place she didn't know. But she held his hand, running ahead of him. Her stomach cramped and roiled as he guided her through alleys and back streets until they were well away from the shooters. He also called the shooting in to the local police.

Finally, they stopped and bent over to breathe, taking in the balmy, humid air. After a moment, Simms lifted her up. They stood behind an ancient live oak that sheltered them like a huge green umbrella. Simms pulled her close and wiped her hair away from her face, his mind swarming with a thousand questions. A thousand wishes.

She stared back at him, the adrenaline falling fast, the awareness spiking through both of them with arrow-like precision.

"Blythe."

Before Blythe could speak, Simms kissed her, his hands holding her cheeks with a tenderness that melted her and calmed her, his kiss telling her the hundreds of thoughts he'd never whisper in her ears or say when he was looking into her eyes.

Blythe wrapped her arms around his back and returned the kiss, letting loose the pain and agony of having a target on her back, of almost losing her life to a madman and his mixed-up schemes, of being an orphan all over again. Her anger changed into a sweet need, the feelings of comfort and security pouring like pure water across her soul. She was still so on fire with anger, but now she felt a new strength giving her renewed life. She'd survive. She'd survive and she'd never forget how it felt to be kissed by a man who always did the right thing, a man who would walk away from her because there could be nothing between them once they were free and clear.

Finally, he pulled back but still held his hands on her face, his own surprise telling her he'd felt something too. "It's going to be okay," he said. "I'll make it okay."

"I know," she replied. Then she kissed him again.

The joy of their unspoken discoveries didn't last long. Simms got a report from one of their details. "Got it," he said after looking grim.

He ended the call and took her hand. "We're on our own now," he told her. "Both cars are damaged and one officer is down but his bulletproof vest saved him. They're with the locals right now, explaining what happened. The SUV got away."

"And the truck?" she asked, still reeling from her anger and that kiss.

"We leave it for now. The locals will tow it in to look for lodged bullets or any other evidence.

I'll have some explaining to do to the Klassens and my captain."

"Did you clear any of this?" she asked, aware that she was fast learning lawman lingo.

"I don't ever clear very much of anything," he admitted. "I do what needs to be done and ask for forgiveness later."

"How's that working for you?" she said as he tugged her up the alley and across tree-shaded hiding places. He was reckless at times, she knew. But he was also alert and confident in what he had to do. She admired that about him.

She would learn to be like that—confident and alert. Her anger pushed its ugly head up again, but she held it in check. There would come a time for more anger. Right now, survival kicked in.

Simms guided her to a corner. "Let's cross over and get lost in the crowds. Then we'll find a way back to the farm."

She wanted nothing more. "I'm going to pray for that. I want all of them to be safe."

"You and me both."

Neither mentioned the kiss they'd shared. Blythe held tightly to the memory of how he made her feel. This had brought out every emotion she'd tried so hard to keep at bay and told her there was so much more to real love than just marrying into money.

So much more.

She wouldn't spoil the memory of these few precious moments by asking him why he'd kissed her. She knew why. Simms needed love like everyone else.

He held her hand tight while he scanned everything and everyone, buildings with balconies, people in shorts and T-shirts and children laughing as their parents handed them ice cream. She could hear the Gulf waters crashing against the shore, tugging and pushing, always roiling and falling back.

Life. She wanted life. "We were supposed to lure them out and we did. What went wrong?"

"Traffic and the timing," he responded. "Our men couldn't get clean shots, and the people in that SUV didn't care who they shot. We think one of them is wounded, so that could bring about some leads."

"We almost got out of here," she replied, her tone full of disappointment. "So close."

Simms's hand tightened on hers. "We will find a way. See that parking garage to the left?"

She glanced over toward the dark bowels of the building where vehicles lined up like June bugs on a sunflower. She didn't like this place, but she'd have to go inside to seek shelter. "*Ja.*"

"We're going to run as fast as we can to that garage. Right now."

They took off across the front entryway of the huge condo decorated with dolphin fountains and lush palms trees and colorful oleanders and hibiscus. Behind them tires squealed and an engine roared, the bitterness of burnt rubber mingling with the salty sea air each time she took a breath.

Blythe didn't dare glance back. The dark coolness of the cavernous garage surrounded them, while engine fumes, gasoline and old dust wafted through the air. Doors slammed and footsteps carried, but they kept running up and around the rows and rows of vehicles.

"Elevator," Simms said in a heavy breath while he motioned to the left.

Blythe hurried to the elevator that would take them up and inside the hotel, her heartbeat matching her pounding tennis shoes. Just as they hit the corner a foot away from the elevator doors, a figure moved in the shadows. Simms yanked her back against a wall and positioned her behind a huge cement column. Putting a finger on his lips, he nodded at her. Blythe held her breath, hoping her pulse wasn't as loud as it sounded in her ears, wishing they could have truly blended in with the crowd.

Simms pulled her close, his gun out, his body shielding hers as he waited. The man shuffled and stomped his feet, his shoes tapping out a warning that brought him closer and closer to where they were hiding. Simms waited and watched until the other person was even with them. Blythe couldn't see him but she could almost envision him sniffing like a rabid animal, waiting for its next kill.

The man moved closer, a grunt of a chuckle echoing throughout the veins of the garage. "Blythe, I know you're in here. I've known your every move. And now you're cornered, with no place to run. You wouldn't listen. You wouldn't cooperate, and we've had to alter our plans."

Simms held her close, his finger on her mouth, the garage now stifling and hot. She prayed she wouldn't cough from the fumes of cars and the stench of evil dancing around this man.

"What? No words? No talking to me. C'mon, aren't you curious about your dear *Aenti* Rita?"

Blythe gasped, the sound softly echoing around her. Then she looked up at Simms and mouthed *"Arthur Glick."*

Simms's expression hardened as he realized the man standing five feet away was her *aenti*'s husband. He silenced her again and tugged her behind him.

"I can take you to her," the voice called out. "Before it's too late."

Blythe twisted, ready to face him and call him out for the liar he was, but Simms held her back.

"And then, there's that pretty little girl with the dog, what's her name—Anna, Angie, *neh*, Agatha. And Bloomer, such a friendly dog. Or at least he was before he ran away."

Blythe tried to get away from Simms, her aim to confront her tormentor, but he refused to let her go. In the next second, her world stood still as Simms twisted and fired at the same time that Arthur Glick lifted his own weapon.

Arthur missed and ducked down out of sight while Simms pivoted and tried to get her to the elevator. Another shot rang out, and this time Simms went down.

Down and on the floor, blood seeping out of his body.

Blythe screamed and fell next to him? "Simms?"

He moaned, lifted his head. "Run."

She grabbed his gun. "I'm not leaving you. I'll shoot him myself."

Simms reached for her hand. "Run…" He looked into her eyes. "I'm sorry."

Then he went quiet, his gaze on her, his eyes slowly closing.

"Simms, wake up. You can't do this to me. You can't leave me."

He didn't move. Was he still breathing?

With a sob, she turned, the gun heavy in her grasp, and aimed it out into the parking garage. "You want me, Arthur? Then show your face!

I'll go with you, but I have no hidden money. Simms is down, and right now, I don't care about anything but keeping Agatha alive."

"Smart woman," Arthur said as he rose from behind a service truck, his gun aimed at her. "C'mon, put the weapon down, Blythe. If you shoot me, they will all die. We're going to visit the orange groves. We'll have us a *gut* talk, and if you behave, the *kinner* will be spared."

"I'll behave," she replied, her heart wrenching at the thought of leaving Simms here to die. But in her mind, she knew she'd fight this man and those who had sent him till the bitter end. She'd fight with all her might to bring them to justice. She wouldn't let Agatha go through what she'd been through. If she could do it, she'd shoot Arthur right now, but he might be the only person who knew where Agatha was.

Nothing else mattered after all.

Because if Simms was dead, how could Blythe keep on living?

SEVENTEEN

Simms woke up with a start, the pain in his arm shooting like a firecracker up to his shoulder. Where was he?

Lifting his head, he realized his hands were tied to what looked like a wooden piling and his feet were tied together.

He was no longer in the parking garage, and he had no idea where to go from here. His pulse jolted with adrenaline while his mind filled with awful memories. The garage, Arthur Glick with a gun, shots fired, Blythe calling his name.

"I'm sorry…"

He thought he would bleed out and die this time, but somehow he'd survived again. Why had they let him live? And why had they brought him here?

His head spun with scenarios until he hit on one that made him sick to his stomach. They wanted to torment him, and the only way to do that was to keep him alive and alone while they did horrible things to Blythe. Which meant she had to be somewhere nearby.

"Blythe?" He screamed her name again. "Blythe, are you here?"

No answer. No lights to show him the way, no footsteps to show him his abductors. He was in total darkness and he didn't know where Blythe was. Simms had never felt this helpless, this alone, this afraid. What had he done?

"Blythe?"

He let out a growl of anger and tried to tug his hands apart, hoping to break the ties around his wrists, but that only brought more pain and chafing rope burns.

Why had he decided bringing Blythe out into the open would be a good idea? He knew better, but he wanted to help the Klassens. He thought he could protect her and yet, she wasn't here with him and he wasn't able to move. His head hadn't been in the game. Because his heart wanted to stay near the woman he'd fallen in love with. To the point that he'd lost focus.

With another angry growl, he twisted and pushed at the ropes holding his hands together, each movement agonizing from the shot he'd taken in his left arm. Whoever had brought him here had done their own kind of damage. His left jaw burned with a familiar pain. They must have knocked him out when he tried to fight them.

Knowing he'd failed slayed him in a way nothing else in his life had ever done. If Blythe was taken, or worse, left for dead, this would be the end of his career because he just wouldn't care about anything if Blythe died in vain.

He looked around, trying to figure out where they'd taken him. But darkness and the struggle to keep from passing out overwhelmed him.

So he lay still, taking in the stars he could see through the hole in the roof, and realized he was in a dilapidated old house somewhere near water. He heard water hitting against the shore, and something else he couldn't quite make out.

Would they leave him here, wounded, to die?

Wait. He heard that noise again. A boat knocking at a dock.

A boathouse. He was in an old boathouse. If he could get away and make that boat work, he'd figure out where he was. Tugging against the tight rope around his hands, he grimaced with pain when he tried to move his left arm. The shot had gone through his upper arm, and the pain burned at him like a hot flame. He was no good, because his arm was bleeding and he was getting weaker by the minute. Where was his phone?

It didn't matter. He was too weak to get to his phone, too weak and defeated to make a move or even call out for help.

He'd have to figure out how to get away before they came back. Because he knew they'd return to finish what they'd started, to humiliate him and make him suffer helplessly while they tried to get Blythe to break. He'd be shark bait by daylight, and he didn't want to think about what might happen to her.

He didn't know how long he'd been here, but the fresh blood oozing out of his wound told him not that long. He was still breathing, so that gave him the little bit of adrenaline he needed. Still he had to try to get his hands untied.

Simms stopped and breathed deeply. "Dear Lord, I know I've been a slacker for so long and You don't owe me anything, but can You show me the way, Lord? Show me how to get to Blythe?"

His whispered words echoed back to him. Had the Lord heard his prayer? Did he have any worth left to ask such a thing?

Please, his mind shouted over and over. *She deserves better than me, I know. But please.*

Glancing around, he saw a big fishing hook dangling off the wall a foot away so he tried to drag himself from the old pillar so he could reach the hook and use it to loosen the ropes digging into his wrists. Each movement sent agony up and down his arm and chest, the pain of an open bullet wound familiar but stronger than he'd remembered before.

I should be dead by now, he thought, his mind playing tricks on him. During his detective years, he'd been shot at many times, stabbed a couple of times, knocked out too many times to count, and now he was tied up and helpless. Helpless when someone he loved really needed him.

Love? Simms stopped and gulped in a breath. He did love Blythe, and now that he'd admitted that to himself, there wasn't anything he could do about it. He might not ever see her again.

"That's a new one," he said out loud, hoping someone would hear him and he could see his captors. "Me helpless, me in love, me praying for help, me and Blythe together." But it could never be, and he had to accept that.

Yet he could still try to save her life and just knowing that gave him strength. He could redeem himself if he managed to stay alive.

"Hey, anyone out there? Let's talk."

Nothing but the lapping of water, which now sounded like laughter mocking him with each push against the old dock. He had to try again, so he studied the rope and realized it was some kind of cheap nylon, now rotten and aged. Simms pushed against the wall then twisted, gritting his teeth as pain fought back against any movement. He touched the old wallboards, hoping to find a loose nail, splinters tickling at his sweaty skin. When he hit something solid, the sting of it pierced his hand, but he smiled. It was a big strong nail hanging on a loose piece of shiplap. "Got you."

Lifting up, he grunted with all his might and placed his tied hands against the massive nail's round head, tugging and pulling as the old threads of the rope began to unravel and give while the nail loosened more and more. This would take a while and he might pass out yet, but if he could catch the nail when it began to fall, he could finish off the other ropes and he might make it out of here alive.

And then he'd make sure these people paid for everything they'd done.

When the nail tore through the frazzled rope around his good hand and fell with precision into his lap, Simms rejoiced and yanked at the ropes, causing both the nail and the torn rope to drop against the nasty damp floor. He grabbed it with his free hand and began to unravel the ropes still around his bleeding arm.

"Done," he said. "Now to get my feet untied."

Simms worked on his feet, the pain in his arm screaming in protest, sweat pouring down his brow, while the humidity only added more moisture to his slippery hands. Finally, the ropes fell away from his feet. He pushed himself up the wall and grabbed the big fishing hook.

He was halfway toward the door when he heard a vehicle approaching and then footsteps stomping against the old dock.

Blythe kept her eyes closed and hoped she could find a way out of this. Her worst nightmare had come back, and this time she would have to survive alone, without anyone's help. Simms was dead and no one knew where she was. She swallowed the bile rising in her throat and opened her eyes. But the image of him lying so still with blood all around him would never leave her mind.

She'd focused on what had to happen next. Arthur had blindfolded her and put her in a big windowless van. She'd tried to estimate how long they'd driven. Maybe an hour or so. Then she'd sniffed familiar scents in the air.

Citrus trees. Ripe citrus fruit. That didn't mean they were back near Pinecraft because Mira had told her there were over two hundred citrus growers in the area.

But she held out hope that if they had Agatha, they hadn't taken her far from home.

"Where is Agatha?" she asked again, her throat raw from begging them to tell her about the little girl. "I need to know she's safe and alive."

Danny Lewis stood over her with a smirk, a flashlight showing her his eerie face. He must have been handsome at one time, but now his expression held a ragged rage, a worn-down frown, and his eyes, so like Hayden's, were full of a spewing hatred. Delusional, that's how he looked.

"Why would you care about a little girl? You're sitting on a goldmine that belongs to me, and you won't tell me how to get to what should be my inheritance."

"I've told you over and over," she said. "I don't know where Hayden hid his money. Most of his assets were frozen when he was indicted for several crimes—murder, transporting contraband and price gouging—to mention a few."

Danny glared down at her, the flashlight casting a yellow light on his face that did not complement him. "You had it all, the good life that I missed out on. Yeah, he sent checks, but just enough to cover the bills. But my long-suffering mom put most of that into an account for me."

"So you have money?" she asked, trying to stall him, trying to find a way out of the cold warehouse where he'd taken her. She could smell the over-ripe citrus fruit—that was the first clue. And he hadn't killed her yet, which meant she had to keep talking and make him slip up.

Praying she was close to Klassen Farm, she

tried again. "If you have money after your mother's passing, why do you need more?"

He leaned so close, she had a flashback of Hayden doing the same thing, which caused her breathing to go shallow. Thinking of Simms and Agatha, she took a deep breath and stared back at him. "I'm sorry, Danny. Your father was a cruel man who kept me prisoner once I found out the truth about him. He wasn't true to the Amish way of life."

Danny tugged at her loose hair. "Now look who's talking? You're not even dressed Amish and your hair is a real mess."

"I was hiding," she said, her patience wearing thin, her mind going to those dark places again. "Hiding from you, Danny. I didn't know you even existed until a few hours ago, and yet you kept trying to abduct me and you will probably kill me once you get what you think I have."

"Well, you *do* know about me now, don't you, sweetheart?" he said, grabbing her arm, his fingers digging into her flesh. "And I think you're lying. Your aunt was full of information, a regular chatterbox."

"What did you do to her?" Blythe shouted, thinking sheer rage would keep her alive, if nothing else.

"She's where she needs to be," he said, stepping back. "Arthur only married her because I promised him a cut. He's still alive because... because he loved my mama."

Arthur and Danny's mother? So her *aenti*'s husband wasn't even Amish.

"Tell me about her," Blythe said, hoping for a reprieve. "My mother died when I was young, and my sister and I went to live with Rita. She was not kind to us, so I can see how she'd want in on any inheritance you think might be out there. She never approved of me, anyway."

"No one approves of you," he shouted, his pacing increasing with every word. "My mother loved Hayden and yet, after all those years of waiting for him to come back, he married you instead. I want to shoot you to honor her, but you have to tell me the truth and give me what's mine. Do you want all the people you love to die because of your greed?"

"My greed?" She stared back at him, wishing he could understand. "I gave up everything to get away from Hayden Meissner. He kept his greediness hidden from everyone. Even you, Danny."

"You had to know he was bad," Danny said. "My mother loved him, and he refused to marry her. But he married you, a woman a few years older than me."

"*Ja*, he did," she said, seeing a crack in Danny's armor. "And he had affairs with other women. He failed at being a true Amish person. And he failed you, too."

"Don't try to butter me up," Danny said. But he sank down onto a rickety chair across from where he had her tied to a support beam. Then he said, "They both failed me. My mother extorted him to get more money, and she withheld that money from me. I got a big inheritance after she died, and I was so angry at both of them. He refused to see me when I tried to visit him, and then Rita went on my behalf and told Hayden what we wanted—that he'd need to give the money over to his only son."

"And after that, he went into a fit of rage, didn't he?"

She could see the sorrow in Danny's eyes, and while she sympathized with him, she couldn't forget what he'd done to her. What his father had done to her. "Danny, was he angry at you? Is that what caused his heart attack?"

Danny didn't look at her. Finally, he wiped his face and nodded. "He told Rita I was nothing to him. A mistake. He said he was tired of being milked by a gold digger. My mother did many bad things, but she felt forced to extort him so she could give me a good life. She only used the money he sent to keep a roof over my head and store up for my future."

"And look how you're using that money she

saved. For what? Chasing people, threatening people and murdering anyone who doesn't do the job. That means you're a lot like him, Danny. Unless you can change."

Danny bolted out of his chair and grabbed her, lifting her up despite the ropes that held her, his dark eyes burning with fire, his hands on her trembling as he shook her. "I'm not here to get a lecture or a therapy session, Blythe. You'd better tell me where the real money is or I'll murder the next person in line. And you know who that will be."

"Simon Bueller."

Simms grimaced and pretended his hands and feet were still tied, the ropes he'd loosened broken and lying where he'd hurriedly placed them back across his hands and feet. It was almost dawn, so he'd have to move quickly to find Blythe. Dana would know they were missing by now, but could she find them in time? Blythe and Agatha first, he hoped. He'd take care of himself. The thought of that sweet little girl in the hapless hands of these greedy people made him so angry he truly believed he'd kill someone.

"Arthur Glick," he shot back. "Did you bring coffee?"

"You don't get to eat or drink," Arthur said,

showing Simms the gun in his right hand. "You've been a thorn in our side since the beginning."

"You mean, since you worked for Hayden Meissner and then left him hanging while you hid out and changed your name?"

Yeah, he'd had a little time to think here all alone, so Simms had put things together and come up with his own conclusions. But was he correct?

"Wow, they told me you were good, but I'm impressed," Arthur replied. "I did work for Hayden, but we had a parting of ways when he realized I was dating the mother of his son. It's not easy, hiding from him."

Points on getting that one right. Simms perked up and went on. "And you decided you'd continue to nurture Danny-Boy after his mother died, correct?"

"I felt it my duty," Arthur said as he strutted around like a peacock, never once checking Simms's ties. "I had changed my name for personal reasons and…since I'd watched Hayden go through the motions of being Amish, I decided I could pretend, too. That's when Danny and I got close. The young man was so easy to manipulate, and he truly deserves his inheritance." Arthur wiped a flick of a spider web off his dark shirt. "I became his mentor and helped him with his bold plan. I really did want to marry Maria—

his mother, but when she died our plan changed. We had to come up with a better one."

"I reckon you did, at that." Simms grunted then gritted his teeth against the pain playing darts with his body. He watched Glick, biding his time. He had the fishing hook, and he might have enough energy to push the older man into the water. "You mean the plan to find Blythe and force her to take you to the hidden treasure?"

"That's the one, only our Blythe is a sneaky little lady. I infiltrated the family, married a woman who whines about everything—"

"And convinced that woman to fall for you and your money, even if you didn't have that money yet."

"See, you are smart. But you're also as gullible as the rest, running around to save poor misunderstood Blythe." Glick stopped strutting and headed toward Simms. "Always the hero, right?"

"Yep, buddy. That's me, always the hero." Even this misguided man had to see how Simms had failed.

Glick cackled with laughter and then leaned in. "You ain't no hero, Simms. You are a menace, and this is the end of the road. We have Blythe and we have Agatha, two people you care about the most, I'm guessing. So we don't need you meddling with us anymore."

"You can take me and return them," Simms

suggested. "We'll talk business. Or let me see them—proof of life and all that."

"See, there you go meddling, coming up with plans. We took a vote and decided you never knowing would do the treat. You being dead will certainly make things easier from here on out."

"I'm not meddling," Simms said in a calm voice. "I'm going to put you both in prison."

"I don't think so," Glick replied. "I'd planned to take you to them, let you watch. But Danny didn't want you there. Too risky. So he told me to do what needed to be done."

Glick lifted his gun and aimed it at Simms.

Simms held the rage boiling over in his bones, and before Glick knew what happened, Simms slid up the wall, hit the other man with the heavy old hook and slammed at the gun to knock it away just as Glick fired. Then he dropped the fishing hook and grabbed Glick by the throat. With a roar of deep anger and pent-up aggravation, Simms kicked the man's gun against the far wall and pivoted with a right hook to the chin and sent Glick flying. Simms then lifted the older man and dragged him toward the gaping door.

Glick tried to twist away, but Simms held tight, ignoring his own burning arm, and pushed him out the door. Then he shoved Glick toward the dark lapping waters of what looked like a small bay. "Tell me where Blythe and Agatha are, or you'll be swimming with the gators."

He waited, heard a splash. "They smell your fear, so talk."

"I don't believe you'll do it," Glick shouted.

Simms pushed him closer to the end of the pier. "Try me."

"Okay, they're in an old warehouse in that swampland on Klassen Farm."

"You'd better be telling the truth," Simms replied. "You wanted me gone. Well, I'm leaving after I tie you up and once I find a place with a phone, I'm calling my fellow officers to take you to jail. Because *you* are a *menace* to *me*."

Yanking Glick back inside, Simms tied him to a strong post and made sure the ropes would stick. Then he hurried to the van Glick had been driving and sighed with relief when he found the keys.

Some people were good at being criminals.

And some didn't have a clue.

Arthur Glick was the clueless kind.

Simms didn't care about Glick right now.

And he really needed to find Blythe and tell her he loved her.

EIGHTEEN

Blythe had to get away and find Agatha. She'd begged, she'd tried to bide her time, and now, she was about to go into a full-blown panic.

"Think," she kept telling herself now that Danny had left her alone again. "A warehouse, the smell of fruit trees, the sound of a vehicle echoing from a distance."

Had they brought her back to the Klassen Farm?

Of course, if they had Aggie, they might have kept the child close to home to avoid anyone knowing.

Blythe went with that theory while she studied her surroundings in the dawn light. A small warehouse, not a shack. But still isolated and a bit chilly. Could it be on the farm?

She struggled with her ropes again, twisting and stretching, the skin on her wrists raw and stinging with pain. She scraped the heavy nautical ropes against the pole they'd tied her to, hoping to frazzle a few threads. When she heard a noise outside, she stopped, fear washing over her like brackish water.

The door popped open and Bloomer came running into the small, dank space, his nose in the air.

"Bloomer?" Tears fell down Blythe's face. "Bloomer, you found me? Where is Agatha?"

Bloomer sniffed at her and licked her cheek. "That's a good boy, but where is Agatha? Where's Aggie?"

Bloomer ran to the door and then back.

"Can you take me to her?"

The dog yelped low, as if he understood.

Desperate now, Blythe held up her tied hands. "Bloomer?"

The dog ran back to her, sniffed the ropes then, to her amazement, started chewing against the ropes. He thought they were playing a game.

Blythe held her breath, praying they could get away before Danny came back and found them. She kept tugging at the ropes and sliding them up and down the rusty pole. When one of the ropes snapped, she gasped with joy.

"Keep at it, Bloomer. Don't stop."

Bloomer looked up at her and then back at the door.

"I know, I know. We have to find Aggie." She tugged at the ropes again. "Help me."

Bloomer went back to tugging as if it were a fun game. Blythe cheered him on, pulling back and playing with him. He growled low while his teeth worked on getting the rope all to himself.

With a growl and one big tug, he pulled the rope loose enough that Blythe could slip one wrist out.

"Good boy," she whispered, tears of joy and relief falling down her face. With a few more tugs the rope unraveled and she finally broke free, falling to her knees to hug Bloomer.

"Thank you," she said, dizziness and fatigue hitting her with a heavy slap. Fighting against that, she pushed her fallen hair away from her face and petted Bloomer on the head. "Now let's get out of here. Take me to Aggie, okay?"

Simms drove up an old trail road away from the water and got on the road. Stopping at the first gas station he could find, he flashed his badge and borrowed the shocked clerk's cell phone to report Glick's location, then he called Dana.

"I'm alive," he said in a weak voice. "Blythe is gone but Glick is in custody. They took her to the swamp near the farm. Where is Agatha?"

Dana let out a sigh. "Oh, I'm so glad to hear your voice. When your detail people reported they'd lost you, we were so worried. Everyone here is okay. We've located Jeff and Adam, and we have them in custody. They were in on this. And Agatha is right here with us, Simms. What's going on?"

"They got to us, said they had Aggie. Shot me and took Blythe. I managed to get the location out of Glick. They hid her on the back side of the farm, probably to stay close in case they did take Aggie. Start a thorough search in the swamp, Dana. I'm on my way."

He handed the phone back to the clerk, then grabbed it again. "Where are we?" he asked the clerk.

"About ten miles west of Sarasota," she said, eyeing the blood from his wound and his dirty clothes. "Do you need help, Officer?"

"Yes, I do. I need a cup of coffee and some pain pills."

"I'm on it."

While the frightened clerk hurried away, he called headquarters and updated his shouting captain. "We have Arthur Glick. I have to go." He gave the location based on how many miles he'd traveled and a couple of signs he'd seen. "I need to hurry, sir. They have Blythe."

The clerk didn't hesitate to bring a huge to-go cup and a bottle of pills to him. Simms gave her a twenty and a quick briefing, each second precious. "You know how it goes," he said as he headed out the door. "Criminals. Left me for dead in a nearby brackish bay, but I survived and caught one of them."

Her eyes became as wide as two sugary donuts. "I guess he deserved it, huh?"

"Yeah." He thanked her for her help. "Stay safe."

She kept staring until he was back on the road. Simms had to think. Arthur Glick had come to kill him, so that meant they were either done with Blythe or they didn't want him as a witness when they killed her. What if they didn't have Blythe at the farm?

Deciding he'd have to start there, Simms gunned the engine and took off. He'd wasted enough time. He had to find her.

Blythe hadn't considered that trying to hide with a big, playful dog might not be the best plan. But Bloomer had saved her, and she trusted him right now more than she did humans. So she checked the outside by peeping through the door, a door she thought Danny had locked. Thankful that the lock hadn't worked, and that Bloomer had managed to shove it open, she pulled the dog along with her, coaxing him to find Agatha.

Then she glanced up and realized where they were. Her heart skipped and skidded as she took in a huge gulp of musky, decaying air.

A swamp. The swamp at the edge of the farm, where they must have been hiding out and watching her every move. Probably where they'd talked to Jeff and Adam and bribed them to help.

Blythe held to Bloomer's collar while the dog glanced up at her with questioning eyes. Then she noticed his legs and paws covered with mud and still damp from the brownish water.

"You came through that, didn't you, boy?"

How had this dog managed to get to her without Danny hearing him or seeing him? Blythe glanced around, taking in the cypress trees and old oaks, the overgrowth and mossy hideouts. If she wanted to get away and find Agatha, she'd have to go through this overgrown marsh.

Danny had left her here for a reason. He knew even if she tried to escape, she would have to go through a dangerous swamp full of predators to reach the other side. And he didn't expect her to do that. She was surrounded on every side by swampland. But where was Agatha?

"What if I'm too late?" she said to Bloomer. "Did you come here looking for Agatha because you know her scent?"

Bloomer's ears lifted at the mention of his favorite person.

"Can you take me to Aggie, Bloomer?"

The big dog barked and did a circle. Then he headed straight. Toward the swamp.

Blythe knew what she had to do. Courage. She needed courage. What would Simms say?

Tears pierced her eyes as she thought about him, lying there so still. Dead. Could it be true? Was Simms dead? She had no idea, and no one would tell her. Danny and Arthur had taunted her and teased her but neither of them had confirmed that Simms was gone. They'd only told her their men had brought her to them. That their men were watching in the woods.

She had no choice now but to go through the swamp to the farm to get help for Agatha. Even if she was too late, she needed to do this. Aggie was innocent, and Blythe had brought this to the family.

She'd end it, once and for all.

"Let's get out of here, Bloomer," she said, letting go of his collar.

Bloomer took off, barked back at her and turned to see if she was coming.

Blythe said a prayer, thought about Simms and headed toward the water. Putting her foot in caused her to step back and then try again. The swamp ran cold and dark with grass and weeds covering her tennis shoes in a decaying dark green slime. Something moved in the water, causing a ripple that tickled her toes.

I can't. I can't.

"Blythe, you know what's in that swamp,

right? You might as well give up and come on back to me."

Blythe pivoted, something slimy slithering across her wet shoes, to see Danny holding a gun pointed at her. "I'm not coming back, Danny."

She turned again, expecting a bullet to hit her, but he only laughed. "Do what you want but right about now, Arthur should be bringing Agatha to see you. I mean, her dog is missing and we know she'll try to find him. Arthur will be waiting for her."

Blythe stopped as the water rose to her waist. Had they purposely sent Bloomer to her, the way they'd obviously made sure he'd be inside the *grossdaddi haus*?

"I thought you had Aggie already," she shouted. "If you show her to me, I'll tell you everything."

What other choice did she have? She needed to see Agatha alive. If she'd learned nothing else from Simms, it was to ask questions for verification before you went anywhere with a criminal.

"She'll be here soon. You can stand there with the gators and snakes or you can come back to me and clean up a bit. I'll send Bloomer to meet them on the trail. The trail that's not actually in the water."

The trail she'd never find, Blythe figured. Bloomer barked and waited. Danny laughed and waved her back.

Somewhere inside her, Blythe felt anger rising up like a burning phoenix that filled her tired, wet, cold body with a heated rage. She glanced at Bloomer then she glanced back at Danny. And she remembered something else Simms had taught her.

Run.

"Go, Bloomer."

Bloomer took off ahead of her, glancing back as she stepped gingerly at first and then ignored the sludge and grass trying to hold her down, and the surprised man screaming at her. Rancid water splashed around her as her tennis shoes tried to sink her in dark grassy mud. Then gunshots rang out.

Danny was trying to shoot her. It was now or never.

Blythe kept going, her body shivering with cold and fear, her mind going to Simms and the kiss they'd shared, the dog guiding her and giving her the strength to continue.

Together, she and Bloomer raced through ancient trees covered with green moss, and splashes that sounded like monsters heading for them.

Don't look back. Don't look back.

Blythe thought she'd die right here. She'd be taken by the dirty, nasty water that held a certain beauty of its own, but also held a kind of death toll to those who dared disturb it. Growing weaker by the moment, she prayed and thanked *Gott* for getting her this far.

Then she heard Bloomer barking a happy bark. Blythe stopped, looked up and saw Agatha hurrying toward the dog, Simms running behind the young girl, the sound of sirens off in the distance.

It had to be a hallucination. And yet, she dragged herself out of the water and fell into the mud with hope in her heart. Simms was coming for her, just as he'd said.

He'd kept his promise.

Blythe woke up in a warm bed that smelled like lavender and rosemary, in a room with an open window where a white curtain lifted in the coastal breeze.

What a sweet dream.

Then she saw him.

Simms, sleeping in a chair that looked small compared to his big body.

"Simms?" she said, her throat raw, her body sore.

He shot up in the same way he had when she'd been in the hospital and took her hand. "Blythe, I'm here."

"Aggie?" she asked, memories flowing over her.

"Is safe and sound. She saved you, Blythe. She heard Bloomer barking in the swamp, and she was going after him when I arrived with the cavalry. She told me where Bloomer had gone then she took off following him." He paused and took a deep breath. "I saw you there in the water and I thought…"

"The same thing I thought when I had to leave you lying there," she replied. "But you're not dead, Simms. And I'm not either. Somehow, we survived."

"We did." He bobbed his head and blinked hard. "You saved yourself."

Blythe pointed up. "He saved both of us."

Simms kept nodding, unable to speak.

Tears gathered in Blythe's eyes and a lump formed in her throat. She could only smile and stare up at him.

"It's over," he said to her silent screams. "Arthur Glick and Danny Lewis are both behind bars. Glick had a run-in with me, but he'll live, and Danny surrendered without a fight then tried to blame Glick. Dana and the team located Adam and Jeff trying to get on a bus out of Pinecraft. They confessed that Danny watched them leaving with Curtis and bribed them at a fast-food restaurant. He promised them money if they'd sneak him onto the farm. He'd been camping on the other side of the swamp while others did his dirty work. Once they heard Curtis was dead because he'd seen Danny's face, they panicked and started talking. Besides, we have DNA evidence against the whole crew. Glick brought people in to help but killed them if they failed. Danny's ex-military so he set up the bomb the night you slept at the big house, and we have DNA to prove that, too. None of these people were very good at covering their tracks."

"And my *aenti*?"

"She's safe. She realized their true plan and got away. She's been hiding out with a cousin in Ohio, who has verified her story. I think she plans to stay there. The poor woman is terrified to venture past the backyard, from what the authorities there reported to us. She thought they'd killed you."

"Am I finally safe?"

"You are," he said. "I have to leave for a while, to take care of some things. Cora says you can stay here as long as you like."

"And what about you, Simms? What's your next move?"

"I'll explain all of that when I get back."

He leaned in, kissed her forehead and whispered, "Yes, I will be back, Blythe. Don't go anywhere, okay?"

"Okay."

She watched as he hurried away. Was this it then? The end of them together? She knew this day would come, but couldn't he have stayed just a while longer?

Cora and Mira came in then and told her how Simms had carried her out of the swamp and they'd cleaned her up and put her to bed.

"You've been sleeping for about twenty-four hours now," Mira said, patting her arm. "Simms came and went and finished off this case as fast as he could."

"But he left me," she said, tears forming again. "I know we can't be together because he won't go back to the plain ways. I just thought we could be friends."

Cora touched her cheek. "Don't underestimate him, Blythe. He is always full of surprises."

She wanted to ask Cora what she meant but a knock at the bedroom door brought in Adina, Nathan and Nathan's *mamm*, Ruth, who was carrying their seven-month-old son, Nate.

"Sister," she said, trying to sit up. Nate giggled.

Adina ran to her and hugged her. "I'm here, finally. I was so worried. Sounds as if you and Simms had one scary adventure."

"We did," she said. "One I'll never forget."

Adina sat down beside her with a knowing smile. "Tell me more."

A week later, Blythe still hadn't heard a word from Simms.

"I guess he's back at work," she said to Mira as they cleaned up the kitchen after supper. "I knew there could be nothing between us, but he left so abruptly."

Mira stopped wiping down the table. "Do you love Simms, Blythe?"

"I do," she admitted. Mira was like another sister to her now. "But…that's our secret."

"Okay," Mira replied, her gaze full of its own secrets. "Oh, I forgot. Agatha wanted you to see the new yearling we bought. He's so adorable, and we thought you'd enjoy feeding him."

Blythe glanced toward the big barn. "Oh, I'd love that. I need to stretch my legs anyway."

She hurried outside, thinking she'd leave soon and find a job in town. But she planned to visit here often.

When she got to the barn, she didn't see Agatha or a new yearling.

Instead, she saw an Amish man standing there, his back to her. A familiar man. Her heart did a little leap. "Simms?"

He turned around and smiled at her. "Blythe."

She ran to him, and he took her into his arms and lifted her off her feet.

"What are you doing? Are you undercover again?"

"No, Blythe." He motioned to a nearby wooden bench and sat her down. "I won't ever have to do that again," he explained. "I quit. I'm not a detective anymore."

"What?" Blythe glanced around, thinking she'd misunderstood. "What will you do then?"

Simms touched a finger to her cheek. "First, I'll tell you that I love you. And second, I'll ask you to marry me." She tried to speak but he held his finger to her lips. "And third, I'll work here on the farm as security and doing whatever needs to be done. Edward offered me the job because he and Cora are getting on and they'd like to travel some. And finally, you will be here with me, I hope, and we'll live in the *grossdaddi haus*—together."

"We will?" She stood up and whirled around. "Does this mean you've returned to the Amish?"

He stood and took her in his arms. "I did— for you, Blythe. For us. I had to clear up some things with the bishop and also…with my *daed*. I went to him, and we had a long talk and made our peace. Oh, and my sister is here, hiding in the big house. Esther can't wait to meet you. She's always wanted a sister."

"I can't believe this," she said, her bruised heart filling with a glowing warmth. "What can I say?"

"Yes?" he replied, his lips hovering near hers. "Can you say yes, Blythe?"

"Yes," she whispered. "*Ja*. Because I love you so much it hurts."

Simms kissed her and then the big house doors

swung open and everyone piled out to celebrate with them, including Bloomer.

Agatha clapped her hands. "He is sweet on her, ain't so?"

They all laughed at that.

"One more thing," he said as the crowd gathered around them, chattering and smiling.

Blythe couldn't stop smiling. "What, more surprises?"

"Just this," he said with a laugh. "You *are* a distraction, a beautiful, fearless distraction. One I hope to keep for a very long time."

"You'll never get rid of me," she replied. "From now on, let's just chase each other."

They hugged, and he held her close again before everyone went inside to give thanks for this beautiful day and the redemption they'd both found.

"A new beginning," Edward said. "*Gott* always has a plan for us."

Blythe looked over at Simms, still unable to believe her world had changed so quickly. "To a new beginning," she replied. "And a new life."

Simms smiled at her. "Together."

Agatha giggled and grinned. "Can we eat all this food now?"

"Prayers for Thanksgiving," Cora replied.

They all lowered their heads and went silent. Simms reached for her hand and squeezed it.

She held tightly to him and thanked *Gott* for giving her the kind of life she'd always dreamed about.

When they all lifted their heads, Aggie clapped her hands. "*Mamm* says we have another wedding to plan."

Blythe looked at Simms. "*Ja*, we sure do."

* * * * *

Dear Reader,

This story changed so much over several edits, I wasn't sure it would ever get published. But Simms needed his own story after showing up in *Disappearance in Pinecraft*, released in May 2024. Throughout the plot changes, adding the suspense, and trying to get it all together, Simms never changed. He is one of those characters who just sticks in your head.

But he needed a heroine who could match him. Blythe, the missing sister of Adina in the previous suspense, wasn't on the pages of that book until the last chapter, but her sister never gave up on finding her. She deserved a fresh start.

Simms and Blythe together, with the backstory and so much angst and trauma, finally got their happy ending. I hope you enjoyed their story. And remember, God never gives up on you.

Until next time, may the angels watch over you.

Always.
Lenora

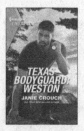